STORM WARNING

Donovan watched the receding blip on the screen and frowned. "Next time, damn you. Next time you're ours."

He stood and stretched, then looked over his left shoulder at Charlie, who had a peculiar expression on his face. "What's with you?"

"I was thinking about what you said, and it worries me."

"What did I say?"

"That *Nemesis* has been playing games with us so far."

"Yeah? So?"

"So what happens when they decide to get serious?"

COMMAND DECISION

J.D. CAMERON

AVON BOOKS ◆ NEW YORK

OMEGA SUB #2: COMMAND DECISION is an original publication of Avon Books. This work has never before appeared in book form. This work is a novel. Any similarity to actual persons or events is purely coincidental.

AVON BOOKS
A division of
The Hearst Corporation
105 Madison Avenue
New York, New York 10016

First Avon Books Printing: April 1991

AVON TRADEMARK REG. U.S. PAT. OFF. AND IN OTHER COUNTRIES, MARCA REGISTRADA, HECHO EN U.S.A.

Printed in the U.S.A.

RA 10 9 8 7 6 5 4 3 2 1

COMMAND DECISION

"Alert stations! All hands to their alert stations!" cried Executive Officer John Percy, initiating a whirlwind of activity on board the U.S.S. *Liberator* as the alarm blared throughout the nuclear-powered submarine. Officers and crew rushed to their respective posts, emptying the mess, the workout room, and the library in seconds. Percy glanced at his superior officer, awaiting further orders.

Seated in his swivel chair behind the helmsman, Captain Thomas P. Donovan surveyed the on-duty personnel already at their positions on the bridge, his mouth set in a grim line. He glanced at the communications officer. "Confirm your readings, Mr. Jennings."

"The readings are accurate, Captain," David Jennings promptly responded. "The ship is slightly over ten miles dead ahead, just sitting there in the water like before. The configuration is the same, too. Narrow beam, about four hundred feet overall. There's no noise. And sonar reports emissions on fourteen-twenty hertz." He looked up, his eyes alight with excitement. "There's no doubt about it, Captain. It's her. *Nemesis.*"

Nemesis! Again! A wave of frustration washed over Donovan and he clenched his fists. After so many days and so many miles, he'd been lulled into a false sense of complacency. He'd actually begun to hope that they'd seen the last of their elusive adversary, especially after the licking *Liberator* had given *Nemesis* off the western coast of the United States, not far from San Francisco. But he should have known better.

"I don't get it," Percy said. "Why is *Nemesis* just sitting there?"

"They're challenging us, Mr. Percy," Donovan stated.

"Sir?"

"They're letting us know that they're back in business, that the damage we inflicted has been repaired, and they're daring us to take them on."

Ever the firebrand, Percy grinned in anticipation. "I say we take them up on their challenge, sir."

"I agree," Donovan said. Here was a chance to end the threat posed by the mysterious sub once and for all, and he wasn't about to let the opportunity pass. "Ahead full! And I want her on the screen."

The screen he referred to was one of three viewscreens that made up the Cyclops display, a three-dimensional image of the ship and its environment. Developed at about the turn of the century and perfected shortly before *Liberator* was constructed, Cyclops served as the tactical eyes and ears of the submarine. By translating and coordinating all of the information received from the sub's sensors, Cyclops could project a holographic representation of the terrain below the vessel, the sea around it, and anything on the surface with startling clarity and realism. And now, on the viewscreens operated by Dave Jennings, on the top screen depicting objects and craft on the surface, materialized a blip representing the *Nemesis,* a blip that resolved itself into the unmistakable contours of the mystery sub.

Donovan leaned forward in his chair. *Nemesis* was similar enough to *Liberator* to be her twin. Both were four hundred feet long. Both had a blister bridge and a distinctive tail bulb. Both were sleek and fast, but so far the *Nemesis* had shown herself to be slightly faster and able to dive to deeper levels.

His mind flashed back to the first contact between *Liberator* and *Nemesis,* about two weeks after World War Three. *Liberator* had missed the fireworks. When the decisions were made and the button pushed to launch the rain of missiles, *Liberator* had been hundreds of feet under the Arctic ice pack, engaging in a test of her ability to stay hidden from enemy detection while observing complete radio silence. Only after two weeks under the ice cap did *Liberator* emerge to find herself in a world gone insane, a world where civilization had been swept away in a fierce nuclear firestorm.

Liberator initially encountered *Nemesis* while en route to Seattle, and the contact had proved inconclusive. *Nemesis* had fled, *Liberator* pursued her, and the phantom sub had outdistanced Donovan and company easily.

Their next confrontation, days later, an hour out of San Francisco, had been more dramatic and potentially deadly. *Liberator* scored a near miss with a torpedo, knocking out the bioacoustical dampening device *Nemesis* used to mask the noise she made, and had nearly taken *Nemesis* down with a Mark 70 torpedo. But once again the enigmatic twin vanished in the depths.

Now it was time for round three.

"Make ready two torpedoes," Donovan commanded.

"The fish are ready to fly," Percy responded.

3

"Target is still dead in the water," mentioned the helmsman, nineteen-year-old Dave Hooper. Of all the men on board, Hooper knew more about *Liberator* than anyone except the systems chief, a big man named Carl Smith. The two of them were frequently found in the mess hall arguing over who could claim to be more knowledgeable.

"She's up to her old tricks," Donovan remarked, studying the Cyclops display.

"The acoustic sensing still indicates emissions on fourteen-twenty hertz," Jennings said.

"Is there any other noise from her yet?" Donovan asked.

"None, Captain."

"Then she's using her damn dampening device again," Donovan snapped. The news confirmed his suspicion that the crew on *Nemesis* had repaired their white noise generator, or whatever the hell it was that effectively prevented *Liberator* from taking reliable readings on different aspects of the enemy craft.

"Target is moving," Jennings declared. "She's diving."

Donovan slapped the arm of his chair in a rare display of anger. *Nemesis* was doing it to them again, drawing them in and then fleeing to depths far below those *Liberator* could withstand. For the umpteenth time he asked himself the same question: Who were those guys? Why was *Nemesis* hounding *Liberator*? There were several rumors popular with different segments of the crew. Percy and the other Commie haters believed that *Nemesis* was a Russian sub, that somehow the Russians had obtained the classified designs for *Liberator* and built a ship of their own along the same lines. Others subscribed to the theory that *Nemesis* might be a second American prototype, constructed in secrecy.

4

A large contingent of the crew was inclined to believe *Nemesis* had been built by the Greater Germany Defense Force. After the two Germanys were unified, the GDF rapidly flexed its muscle, seeking to become a major player on the world stage. It was a known fact that the United States had reportedly scrapped plans to build a second Omega-class nuclear submarine, leaving *Liberator* the distinction of being the one and only, and sold the keel and a partial hull to the GDF. Was it possible, then, that Germany had built its own Omega-class sub at its leased shipyard in Gdansk?

One fact was certain, a fact Donovan found particularly disturbing. During the second encounter, when *Liberator* knocked out the white noise generator, Communications Officer Jennings had been able to run a screw signature match on *Nemesis*. The match had shown Nemesis to have the *exact same* screw signature as *Liberator*. Identical in every respect.

"Are we still at five hundred feet, Mr. Hooper?" Donovan inquired absently.

"Aye, Captain."

"Take her down to one thousand and level off."

"Yes, sir."

"Mr. Jennings, what is *Nemesis* doing?"

"Still diving, Captain. She's at two hundred feet, and she'll cross our bow from port to starboard."

Donovan locked his eyes on the screen. "Mr. Hooper, keep closing as we dive. I don't want to lose her again."

"Closing, Captain," Hooper replied, his tone betraying his youthful zeal.

"Laser to weapons status," Donovan ordered, and felt a tingle run along his spine. The strategy had worked last time, so maybe it would work again.

The sophisticated state-of-the-art laser technology incorporated into *Liberator* was a unique sys-

5

tem. There were two laser turrets, one mounted fore and one mounted aft on the tower. They could be used against surface and submerged targets as a weapon up to a range of one thousand yards. Designed primarily to disrupt electrical circuits, they had been used in combat only once. At extended ranges up to ten thousand yards, the laser system functioned as an effective information probe. When the laser was tied into the Cyclops information-display viewscreens in the probe mode, pinpoint accuracy could be achieved on the location of other ships, thermoclines, or even floating debris.

"Mr. Percy, switch off active sonar when we have a laser lock."

"Aye, Captain," the executive officer answered eagerly.

"Leveling off at one thousand feet," Hooper stated.

"Let me know when the range is thirty-five hundred yards," Donovan said. "I don't want to waste a fish this time."

The distance between the two subs narrowed rapidly, and the image of *Nemesis* on the screen grew correspondingly larger and larger.

"Target is leveling off," Jennings declared. *"Nemesis* is at one thousand feet."

"Good," Donovan said.

"She's turning to port, Captain."

"You heard, Mr. Hooper. Stay on that mother," Donovan directed.

"Like glue, Captain."

"Any new readings, Mr. Jennings?"

"She's bearing two-seven-two and making thirty knots. No, forty knots," Jennings said, and stiffened. "Wait a minute. A new reading, sir. Fifteen hundred hertz."

"Damn," Donovan swore. The familiar pattern was repeating itself.

6

"Target is increasing speed. Fifty knots and rising. I'm still not getting any engine or screw noises," Jennings reported.

"Flank speed, Mr. Hooper. Get us within firing range," Donovan instructed.

"Aye, Captain. Flank speed. Range is slightly under eight miles and closing."

Donovan's abdomen constricted into a knot. Given the superior speed *Nemesis* possessed, getting within firing range seemed unlikely. And he wanted that sub so damn bad, he could almost taste it.

"She's doing it to us again, huh brother?" stated a new voice from directly behind Donovan's chair.

"Hello, Charlie." Donovan greeted his younger sibling without taking his eyes from the screen. "Where have you been?"

"Here the whole time," Charlie replied, staring at the Cyclops display in undisguised fascination. To him, the technology utilized in the holographic visualization was uncanny, almost unreal. He wasn't a regular member of the crew, and his presence on *Liberator* could be attributed to a stroke of luck. He'd been on a helicopter over the Bering Strait when the war erupted, and his chopper had been downed by the same phantom sub his brother now pursued. Of the three crewmen on board the old HH-2G LAMPS helicopter, only he had survived. The emergency locator beacon in his life raft had drawn *Liberator* to him, and he could still vividly recall the overwhelming relief and surprise he had felt when he was lifted from the rescue boat and laid eyes on his brother. After weeks on *Liberator,* he'd grown somewhat accustomed to the routine, if not the technology, but he still missed his life as an airborne ASW technician.

"Target is at sixty-eight knots," Dave Jennings said.

7

"Give me an update, Mr. Hooper," Donovan said to the helmsman.

"We're at sixty knots, Captain. Range is now almost nine miles."

"Yep. We're definitely losing her," Charlie interjected.

"Who made you a sub expert?" Donovan asked testily.

"Hey, don't take out your feelings on me. I've learned a lot since you brought me on board. You said yourself that *Nemesis* is faster than *Liberator*. I'm just stating the obvious."

As if to substantiate Charlie's remarks, Hooper suddenly announced, "Target has pulled away to nine miles and gone to fifteen hundred feet."

"Double damn," Donovan muttered.

"Tough break," Charlie said.

"Maybe not so tough," Donovan responded. "We now know that she's scared of us."

"How do you figure?"

"The last two times we ran into her, *Nemesis* flaunted her power and speed. She let us get close enough to fire torpedoes, to use the laser. But not this time. She wasn't taking any chances. She let us know she was back in the ball game, then took off as soon as we approached," Donovan said. "I'd say whoever is on that sub has learned their lesson. They're not about to play games with us anymore."

"The million-dollar question," Charlie quipped. "Whose sub is she? The Russians? The Germans? Maybe Tibet launched its own sub when nobody was looking."

"Tibet?" Donovan snorted. "Tibet is a dinky little country north of the Himalayas. It's landlocked to boot."

Charlie sighed and touched his brother's right shoulder. "Where's your sense of humor, Tom?"

"It died when the world did," Donovan replied,

then glanced at the helmsman. "Status, Mr. Hooper?"

"Target is well over nine miles away. Sixty-eight knots. Presently at two thousand feet and still diving."

Donovan sat back in his chair and scowled. There went the ball game. "Reduce speed to one-half, Mr. Hooper. Continue to track the target, gentlemen. And feed all the new data into the Cray."

"There isn't much new data, Captain," Jennings said.

"We'll take what we can get," Donovan responded. He held scant hope that *Liberator*'s Cray-9 computer would come up with anything useful, but he had to try.

The designers had equipped *Liberator* with a system for recording everything from military action to cartography. The information was computerized and fed into the Cray computer banks. Every tidbit of data from the external sensors—from radar, sonar, lasers and radio—was recorded digitally and saved. The data banks also contained a videotape recorder that kept tabs on the science labs, and there were cameras mounted on the blister to record *Liberator*'s surroundings.

"Switch the laser from weapons status to probe," Donovan said.

"Aye, Captain," Jennings answered.

Donovan watched the receding blip on the screen and frowned. "Next time, damn you. Next time you're ours."

"Who *are* they?" Percy asked of no one in particular.

Hooper said, "Target is ten miles away and has reached twenty-five hundred feet."

"Slow to one-quarter and continue on our original course," Donovan said. He stood and stretched, then looked over his left shoulder at Charlie, who had a peculiar expression on his face. "What's with you?"

"I was thinking about what you said, and it worries me."

"What did I say?"

"That *Nemesis* has been playing games with us so far."

"Yeah? So?"

"So what happens when they decide to get serious?"

2

He found her in the sick bay with her brother, manning a computer terminal, her pert nose almost pressed to the screen. "What are you doing, Alex? Researching our *Playgirl* archives?"

Alexandra Fisher glanced up from her work and smiled. "Cute, Donovan. Real cute." She ran her right hand through her curly black hair. "You only have *Playboy* on file. I've checked. And I'm busy now helping Peter with his cure for the radiation poisoning."

Donovan gazed at her twin brother, who sat at another terminal nearby, his long hair tied in a ponytail and tucked under his white smock. "Any progress, Pete?"

"A little here, a little there," Peter said, straightening. "The cure won't come overnight, but we'll find one eventually. This equipment you have is astounding. I never expected to find such an advanced medical facility on a submarine. The ROM diagnostics capability alone is priceless."

"You have to remember that *Liberator* wasn't built strictly for warfare," Donovan reminded him. "Part of the justification for her budget was that she would be used for scientific as well as military purposes."

11

"I know. But this ship still boggles my brain. I could lose myself in your library for a year."

Donovan smiled. "I know what you mean."

The library contained a veritable wealth of information. It was stocked with computers, storage devices, and monitors, but no books. Virtually anything a person wanted to read could be brought up on a monitor at the touch of a key. The material in the archives included history, science, literature, art, sports, and more. All the latest technical and scientific journals had been included. Specs on all American warships of the late twentieth century as well as everything known about foreign navies, both hostile and friendly, were also on file.

Donovan glanced from brother to sister, thankful he had brought them on board at San Francisco. Before the war, Alexandra had been employed as a computer wizard and Peter as a surgeon and medical researcher. Together with their father, they had organized an effective resistance against the scavengers and white-shirts who proliferated after society disintegrated. Their father had stayed on to help rebuild the city, but Alex and Peter had yielded to Donovan's persuasive argument that on the *Liberator* they would be able to assist in rebuilding more than a single city—they could contribute meaningfully to the restoration of the world.

One of their major tasks, to which they had already devoted many hours, involved finding a cure for the widespread radiation psychosis. Not only had more people survived the nuclear holocaust then prewar projections had indicated, but a staggering percentage of those who did survive had developed fever, sores, dementia, paranoid delusions, and hyperaggressive behavior: an acute, violent form of radiation insanity that rendered them extremely dangerous.

"We're still working on isolating the specific

agent responsible for the insanity," Alex mentioned. "And I believe we're on the verge of a breakthrough."

"I love an optimistic woman," Donovan said.

Alex looked at him and grinned impishly. "Oh really? Prove it."

"I thought you were engrossed in your work."

"All work and no play makes Alex a bitch on wheels."

"You're aboard a sub."

"Quit nitpicking," Alex said. She stood, her shapely figure swelling her smock in all the right places, and said over her left shoulder, "Hold down the fort, Pete. I'm taking a break."

"Knock yourself out," Peter suggested.

Donovan and Alex left the sick bay and made for the officers' quarters, located forward of the bridge. On the way they passed through the rest of the complex in which the sick bay was located, which included the library, the workout room, and the galley. The crew quarters were forward of the complex, adjacent to the torpedo room and the bow sonar pocket.

Liberator had been designed to spend extended periods submerged, and accordingly ample living space had been a priority. While conventional submarines were renowned for their narrow passageways and cramped quarters, *Liberator* resembled a cruise ship more than a warship with her spacious compartments and comfortable quarters. Each member of the crew had his own cabin, and the officers were privileged to have their own showers and heads.

Donovan took a pack of Lucky Strikes from his shirt pocket.

"When are you going to quit that disgusting habit?" Alex asked, eyeing the cigarettes with the

13

same degree of appreciation she might bestow on toxic waste.

"When I run out," Donovan said.

"I heard the alarm," Alex mentioned. *"Nemesis* again?"

"You must be psychic."

"Anything new?"

"The same old fun and games," Donovan said bitterly, lighting his smoke.

"What are they trying to prove?"

Donovan inhaled deeply. "I wish I knew. They seemed to be playing cat and mouse with us. If they persist, sooner or later they'll make a mistake and we'll nail them."

"Do you think *Nemesis* will follow us all the way to the islands?"

"I wouldn't be surprised," Donovan replied, thinking of the search they were about to conduct for a Pacific island they could use as a base. Originally they had planned to begin their search with the Society Islands, but Donovan had decided to start with the Marshall Islands instead, then head southeast if necessary, conducting a sweep of every island in the South Pacific if that was what it would take to locate a suitable haven.

"Has anyone given you grief over locating the base in the Pacific instead of along the U.S. coast?" Alex inquired.

"Some of the crew prefer basing our operations in the States. Chief Smith is one of them. But the majority of the men are behind me one hundred percent," Donovan said, his forehead creasing as he contemplated their impending course of action. "We need a secure base. That's our paramount concern. And the States is out of the question because of the white-shirts and the looters. We can't be secure if we have to be on alert twenty-four hours a day, which is what would happen if we picked a spot along the coast."

"You don't need to convince me," Alex said. "Our projections indicate the South Pacific came through the war relatively unscathed. The radiation should be well under tolerance levels. I can't predict what the flash effect might have done to the native populations, but the growing and living conditions should be ideal."

"I hope you're right. We'll need a local food supply to keep our ship's stores replenished."

"Not to mention the benefits of a hospitable climate."

Donovan chuckled. "Yeah. I can't wait to see you in a grass skirt."

"Only if you wear a sarong."

"The natives would laugh themselves silly," Donovan said. He looked up as a big man approached. "Hi, Flaze."

"Captain. Alexandra," Systems Chief Carl Smith responded. The chief engineer and acknowledged expert on *Liberator*'s propulsion system and structural design, his nickname had been created by combining "fat" and "lazy." He was a devoted family man, and he had taken the presumed loss of his wife and kids in San Diego hard. "I'm on my way to the library to do some research on *Nemesis.*"

"I wasn't aware there is any data in our library on our twin," Donovan commented.

"There might not be. But this morning I recalled this article I saw in one of the scientific journals that might have a bearing on her identity."

"What was the article about?"

"I can't remember the exact details," Smith said. "But I have this feeling, as if the article might be important."

"Well, let me know if you find anything."

"Will do, Captain," Smith said, and headed forward.

"Interesting," Alex remarked, following Donovan toward his quarters.

"Flazy has become obsessed with discovering the identity of the people behind *Nemesis*. Hooper, too, for that matter. They've spent every spare minute in the library, poring over the archives, hoping they'll stumble across a clue."

"Sounds as if they're searching for the proverbial needle in a haystack," Alex said.

"You never know," Donovan replied. "Besides, it's all we've got for now. Until we acquire more data, we'll be at a distinct disadvantage."

"We should look at the bright side."

"Ms. Optimistic strikes again," Donovan said. "What bright side are you talking about?"

"So far, the only other warship we've run into has been *Nemesis*. Except for her, we seem to have the ocean all to ourselves."

"There are bound to be other warships out there somewhere," Donovan observed.

"Maybe not. Remember that carrier task force you were telling me about? The *Roosevelt* and her escorts were little more than melted slag. Any surface ship caught by the flash effect is bound to be in the same condition."

"We'll see," was as far as Donovan was willing to commit himself on the subject.

They came to the captain's cabin and Donovan opened the door for her.

"My. What a gentleman," Alex quipped, sashaying in an exaggerated fashion over to a plush chair where she took a seat.

"All the Donovan men are courteous to women. Our mother saw to that," Donovan said, closing the door.

"Was she the dominant influence during your childhood years in New York City, Tom?"

"Not really," he answered as he walked over to her. "She was real big on table manners and how to behave in polite society. All that jazz. But my dad was my main influence. I mean, when you're a small boy being raised by one of New York's finest police detectives, constantly hearing about his acts of heroism and his adventures with pushers, pimps, murderers, and other degenerates, you're going to come away from it all with a zest for the adventurous life."

"How in the world does a boy growing up in New York City develop a hankering for a life at sea?"

"My dad again. The old man had a boat that never left the dock, but it was a lot of fun to go there and lounge on the bow and listen to music or gaze at the clouds . . . whatever," Donovan related, a wistful tinge to his voice. "I used to lie on the *West Wind*, dad's yacht, and dream of exotic adventures in foreign ports. I guess some of that stuck with me later when I decided to enter the Navy instead of becoming a priest."

"A priest?" Alex blurted.

"Yeah," Donovan said, somewhat sheepishly. "When I was thirteen, I seriously toyed with the notion of entering the priesthood. The mother superior wanted me to go into the Church. Even as a kid I had this idea in my head that I could make a difference in the world, that I could do some good. She tried to convince me that I could do the greatest good as a priest, saving souls." He paused. "But the life of a priest didn't appeal to me. There wasn't enough excitement in duties like conducting mass and hearing confessions. I wanted something more."

"Sinbad the sailor."

Donovan laughed. "Something like that. I wanted

17

to see the world, to experience life in the raw. At first I thought I would end up on a surface ship, a battleship, a destroyer, one of the big guns. I never expected to wind up on a sub."

"Me neither," Alex said.

"Have you always been into computers?"

"Always. My father was wonderful in that respect. He encouraged Peter and me in the sciences. Unlike most of our childhood peers, we grew to like science and math and all that 'egghead stuff.' I suppose that made me a bit of an introvert when I was younger."

"You? I find that hard to believe. You're so independent, so self-confident."

"My father's influence again," Alex said, and pursed her lips. "He was an Army surgeon once, you know, and later he became an Episcopalian priest. He instilled in us a love for the intellectual life, a desire to care for others, and, most important, a sense of responsibility for our own decisions."

"You must miss him," Donovan commented, and instantly regretted his tactlessness.

Alex's features clouded. "Yes, I do. Peter does, too. But we both feel we'll see our father again someday, so what's the use of moping?"

"At least you know your dad is still alive," Donovan said, reflecting on the probable fate of his father in New York City. The Big Apple must resemble molten apple pie.

Alex looked up at him, her eyes hooded, and ran her right hand down his leg. "So tell me, Sinbad. How much time do you have before you must return to the bridge?"

"I have all the time in the world," Donovan answered. "This ship can practically run herself."

Which was almost the truth. The main advance of *Liberator* over the San Diego class of submarines lay in the extent to which her systems were automated. When on automation, *Liberator* required a minimal on-duty crew to monitor key indicators. Where a typical nuclear sub might have a complement of 120 men or more, *Liberator* managed with only 45 men who worked in three shifts of 15 men each. Because the automation systems were critical to the ship's functioning, the computer and systems-repair crews were the best in the Navy.

The consolidation of crew and monitor position even extended to the command structure. *Liberator* used a section structure with the duty officers in each section reporting to the designated bridge officer. Reactor Control reported to the systems chief. The torpedo room reported to Weapons Control, which in turn reported to the executive officer. Communications embraced Sensors, Computers, and Research. The few overlapping areas, such as the lasers, which could be employed as a weapon or as a probe, were shared. The lasers were the joint responsibility of Weapons Control and Sensors.

Alex smiled seductively. "I could use a back rub."

"Your wish is my command."

Just then the intercom crackled with the voice of Executive Officer Percy. "Captain to the bridge! Multiple contacts off the starboard bow."

Donovan sighed and walked to the door. "Remind me to have Percy walk the plank."

3

"What have we got?" Donovan queried as he sat in his swivel chair.

"Seven contacts, Captain," Percy informed him. "Eight miles off. Bearing two-eight-two."

"Mr. Hooper, come to course two-eight-two and bring us to periscope depth. Let me know when we're within visual range."

"Two-eight-two, and coming to periscope depth, sir," the helmsman replied.

"What can you tell me, Mr. Jennings?" Donovan asked.

"They're dead in the water, but they're not dead, Captain."

"Explain."

Communications Officer Jennings scrutinized a meter on his right. "I'm registering concentrated heat generation on board several of the ships."

Donovan leaned forward. "Engines?"

"No, Captain. I'd say heaters or lanterns, or else someone has set fires on board."

"Put them on the screen," Donovan commanded. He watched a series of blips materialize on the horizon.

"Each ship is two hundred feet in length," Jennings stated.

"The same size as that Japanese trawler we saw."

20

"A Japanese fishing fleet, you think?" Percy asked.

"Could be. Japan had one of the largest on the globe. Almost half a million ships afloat, as I recall. We'll know in a minute."

Minutes later Helmsman Hooper called out, "Periscope depth and close enough for visual, Captain."

"Raise periscope and the antenna mast," Donovan ordered. He checked his watch. Only 1000 hours.

Once the radar-receiving mast had been elevated, Communications Officer Jennings employed the radar receiver to determine if there were any signals from the ships. "No signal readings, Captain."

Nodding, Donovan peered through the periscope at the small fleet. He pressed a button so everything he viewed would be videotaped. Sure enough, the ships were similar to the fishing boat *Liberator* had run into before. That ship had turned out to be little more than a scorched hull adrift at sea. These were in much better shape. Their masts were gone, and there were scorch marks on the decks and wheelhouses, but overall the fishing boats were seaworthy. The big question concerned whether there might be Japanese fishermen on board. He saw no sign of life. But there was only one way to find out for certain. "Mr. Percy, we're going to surface and investigate. Sound alert stations, if you please."

"Aye, Captain," Percy stated, smiling, and pressed the button that activated the alarm heard throughout the sub. Monitors strategically located in the living quarters, the work spaces, and the corridors displayed a message for all the crew to see, which was programmed by the communications officer, Jennings, and read: "Multiple contacts off the starboard bow. Japanese fishing fleet."

21

Alex and Charlie came onto the bridge and took up positions near the swivel chair.

"Mr. Percy, I'll be taking a boarding party onto the nearest trawler. Chief Smith, Alex, and the first gunnery officer will be going with me."

"Begging your pardon, Captain. I'd like to go along."

"Sorry, John. Not this time," Donovan replied. He looked at Jennings. "Are those trawlers hot? Will we need radiation-protection suits?"

"Negative, sir."

"Mr. Hooper, bring us alongside the first fishing boat."

"Aye, Captain."

Donovan swung toward his brother. "You can break out the weapons, Pirate."

"Four?" Charlie asked, his tone tinged with excitement.

"Three. Alex will carry a video camera to record whatever we find."

"See you topside," Charlie said, and exited the bridge.

Smiling at Charlie's transparent eagerness, Donovan watched his brother depart. He'd bestowed the title of First Gunnery Officer upon Charlie because Pirate happened to be one of the best shots in the Navy. Twice Charlie had been the Navy pistol champ, and he loved guns.

"Where'd your brother ever get a nickname like Pirate?" Alex inquired.

"He adopted it after seeing *Raiders of the Lost Ark*," Donovan disclosed. "A seaplane pilot in that flick had the words 'Air Pirates' on the back of his shirt."

Alex grinned. "Pirate and Sinbad. Quite a team."

Donovan turned his attention to the 'scope, scrutinizing the fishing fleet as Hooper brought the sub to within boarding range. He failed to detect a trace of life. "Down 'scope," he directed. "Surface."

The teal-colored hull of the *Liberator* broke water gracefully, and within two minutes the boarding party, Percy, and four armed crewmen were on the foredeck. The boarding party and the crewmen all carried the same type of weapon, the new Navy version of the Luigi Franchi 9-mm automatic. The compact submachine gun sported a 32-round box magazine and could fire 250 rounds per minute. For over a decade the Franchi had been the weapon of choice for leftist guerilla groups in Africa, Latin America, and Southeast Asia because of its reliability and rugged construction.

A four-man raft was placed in the water, and Donovan, Charlie, Alex, and Chief Smith quickly climbed into it.

Percy stood on the starboard diving plane, gazing warily at the trawler. "Be careful, Skipper. We'll cover you as best we can."

"You do that," Charlie spoke up. "I've got a bad feeling about this."

Donovan glanced at his brother, disturbed. Past experience had taught him the value of Charlie's intuitiveness. If Charlie sensed there might be trouble, then there damn well would be trouble. He wondered if he was doing the right thing by bringing Alex along, but it was too late to change his mind. "Let's go," he said.

They paddled the dozen yards to the trawler, which lay perfectly still in the quiet sea. A fishing net hung over the port side within four feet of the water, rendering the use of grappling lines unnecessary. Charlie went up first and fast, and he stood guard on the deck while the others joined him.

"This is spooky," Alex whispered.

Donovan had to agree. The door to the wheel-

23

house stood wide open. Except for a pile of nets and a few scattered tools, the deck was barren. A fishy odor permeated the air.

"Somebody is home. I just know it," Charlie declared. He moved toward the wheelhouse.

"Flaze, you stay with Alex," Donovan ordered, and followed his brother. They peered into the wheelhouse and discovered everything in apparent order. One of the glass panes had been shattered and another was cracked, But otherwise little damage had been done.

"We've got to go below," Charlie said, clearly not enthused by the idea.

Together they walked to a companionway and descended carefully. At the base of the stairs a flickering lantern hung on a gray hook. The brothers exchanged glances and advanced along the narrow corridor. After the luxurious accommodations on *Liberator,* the confined space in the trawler seemed particularly constricting, almost claustrophobic.

A dozen yards ahead a door hung ajar, and light emanated from the room beyond.

Donovan slowed, gripping the Franchi tightly. He nearly gagged when a disgusting, putrid stench assailed his nostrils. Halting, he pressed his left sleeve over his nose and saw Charlie do the same. He'd smelled the rank stink of death before, but never as bad as this. Dreading the sight he would find, he advanced to the doorway.

They were stacked neatly like plates on a shelf, one on top of the other, from the floor to the ceiling. There were eight Japanese seamen, and they had died horrible deaths, their throats slit or their chests and abdomens cut to ribbons. Blood and bodily fluids had seeped onto the floor and formed a foul pool, congealed now into a reddish, oily film. Shriveled intestines dangled from the right side of the man on top.

Donovan felt his stomach start to heave. He staggered a few yards down the passage, and fought the urge to retch. A hand fell on his right shoulder and he jumped inadvertently.

"Are you okay?" Charlie asked.

Donovan gulped and nodded. "Doesn't that get to you?"

"Sure. But after seeing what those wolves did to that crowd in San Francisco, I can handle it."

"The next time I board a ship like this, I think I'll bring nose plugs."

They continued deeper into the trawler, passing several lanterns, only two of which were lit. Eery shadows danced on the walls. Sibilant whispers seemed to issue from the murky corners. The fishy odor became stronger as they neared the hold.

Donovan inspected a cabin they found, a clean room containing a small bunk and a wooden table on which rested a bowl of raw fish and cooked rice. He stuck his finger in the bowl and found the rice warm to the touch. The short hairs at the nape of his neck tingled. "There's definitely someone home," he whispered.

Charlie nodded, then stiffened. "Listen!"

Donovan cocked his head, and it took a moment for him to distinguish the low, raspy laughter emanating from the bowels of the vessel. The laughter rose in volume, then tapered off.

"God!" Charlie exclaimed.

"I feel as if I'm in a Boris Karloff movie," Donovan commented nervously.

"Just so Frankenstein doesn't pop out of the woodwork," Charlie said.

They moved along the gloomy corridor until they reached another flight of narrow metal stairs. Below them yawned a black pit, an inky expanse of emptiness, from which wafted an intensified aroma of fish.

Donovan scanned the chasm and deduced they must be at the hold. He thought of the laughter and wondered if there might be someone down there, watching them. His skin felt as if it wanted to crawl from his body. What if there were white-shirts on board? he asked himself, and the question provoked a torrent of memories.

Liberator's crew had encountered the dreaded white-shirts several times since the war. The first incident occurred in the Aleutians, at Dutch Harbor on Unalaska Island. Donovan and a landing party were attacked by four of the demented bastards. Later, near Seattle, a man in a Boston Whaler attempted to attack the sub while armed with only a shotgun. Then, in San Francisco, Donovan and company had to contend with an army of white-shirts who were determined to wipe out the few normal survivors. The desperate situation had called for drastic measures, and Donovan had called up a Mark 97N to obliterate the white-shirt headquarters. Used during the nuclear shelling of the Andean coke fields ten years before the war, the Mark 97N carried a field-grade nuclear warhead.

No one knew exactly what caused normal survivors to transform into crazed white-shirts. The prevailing medical theory attributed the transformation to radiation insanity. Many of the survivors simply became hopelessly psychotic. But the psychosis alone failed to explain certain puzzling aspects about the white-shirts. Why, for instance, did they all wear white shirts or some semblance thereof? Why did they go around meticulously collecting bodies and burning the corpses? And why did the white-shirts attack anyone who wasn't a white-shirt?

Donovan stared at the black abyss and pondered. Surely there couldn't be white-shirts on board the trawlers? Perhaps several of the crew had gone off

26

the deep end, their sanity shattered by the horror of the nuclear holocaust. That didn't necessarily mean they would become white-shirts, did it? He sighed in frustration. There were too many questions and not enough answers.

Charlie knelt and peered into the darkness. "Should we go down?"

"Not by ourselves. We'd be inviting grief," Donovan said. "Let's return to Alex and Flaze."

They quickly retraced their route, and they both smiled when they finally saw the sunlight streaming down the companionway to the deck.

"I never knew sunshine could look so good," Charlie said.

Donovan opened his mouth to reply when a maniacal laugh rent the air to their rear. He whirled, levelling the Franchi; and it was well he did, for there, less than twenty feet away, stood a scrawny Japanese fisherman attired in filthy black pants and nothing else. His face and chest were caked with grime and crimson stains, his black hair oily and plastered to his head. In each hand he held a slender ten-inch knife, the kind used to slit the belly of a fish with consummate ease.

The Japanese, his brown eyes wide and unfocused, smirked and waved the knives in circles.

"Hello," Donovan greeted him, attempting to communicate but feeling foolish doing so. "I'm Captain Thomas Donovan of the U.S.S. *Liberator.*"

Snickering, the fisherman tilted his head and uttered a string of words in his native tongue.

"We mean you no harm," Donovan said.

Without warning, the Japanese hurled his emaciated frame at the Americans, both knives upraised for a fatal thrust.

Charlie shot him. The burst chattered short and sweet, and the rounds caught the man in the torso

27

and hurled him from his feet to crumple on the floor in a heap.

Donovan edged toward the fisherman, the eight-inch Franchi barrel pointed at the Japanese. He saw blood oozing from holes in the man's back, saw that the chest had ceased moving, and knew the man was dead.

"Do you think he killed all the others?" Charlie asked.

Before Donovan could respond, from the deck outside came a screech and the blasting of Chief Smith's Franchi.

Donovan and Charlie burst from the companionway onto the deck and froze in their tracks, riveted
by a nightmare in progress. There were five Japanese, all scantily attired, all filthy and wielding
various weapons, attacking Chief Smith and Alex.
Two other fishermen were already dead, prone in
spreading puddles of their own blood. But the main
focus of Donovan's attention shifted to Alex. She
was grappling on the deck with a skinny man who
was trying his damnedest to bash in her skull with
a short club.

"Look out!" Charlie cried, and fired at a scare-
crow figure about to pounce on Chief Smith.

Heedless of his safety, Donovan ran to Alex just
as the fisherman succeeded in pinning her on her
back. The man tittered and lifted his club overhead. Donovan never slowed, and he held his fire
for fear of accidentally striking Alex. Instead, he
kicked the Japanese full in the face and knocked
the man to the deck.

"Tom!" Alex exclaimed in relief.

Donovan reached down, grabbed her right hand,
and hauled her erect.

The fisherman carrying the club pushed himself
to his knees and took a wild swing at them.

Without the slightest compunction, Donovan squeezed off a half dozen shots.

Struck in the chest, the skinny Japanese flipped onto his back, convulsed, gurgled, and abruptly expired.

Donovan surveyed the deck, surprised to discover the battle over. Charlie and Chief Smith had disposed of three more of their assailants, and the one fisherman still alive had opted to flee. The Japanese was sprinting toward an open hatch at the bow.

Charlie raised his submachine gun. "I have a clear shot."

"Don't," Donovan stated.

"Why not? He has it coming."

"And who appointed you his judge and executioner?" Donovan countered. His gaze alighted on the video camera, lying several feet away, its casing cracked. "Damn. What happened?"

"They jumped us." Chief Smith related the obvious, his expression betraying the fact he had been rattled by the attack.

Alex nodded at the hatch, through which the lone fisherman had just dropped. "They came up out of there and crawled up on us while we were watching for you. We'd heard shots. If you hadn't arrived when you did . . ." She left the statement unfinished.

"Let's get the hell out of here," Charlie suggested.

"I second that," Chief Smith said.

"To the raft," Donovan ordered.

Alex retrieved the video camera, and staying close together they stepped to the side of the trawler.

John Percy spotted them and bellowed across the gulf separating the ships. "Captain! Are you all right? Do you require assistance?"

"Negative," Donovan yelled back. "We're returning to *Liberator*. If anyone else shows his head, shoot to kill."

"Aye, Captain."

Donovan saw the executive officer bark orders to the four crewmen, who trained their weapons on the trawler with renewed concentration. "Alex and Flaze, you go down first," he directed. "Pirate and I will cover you."

But the fishermen, if there were any left on board other than the one who had fled, did not bother the boarding party again. Before long they were off the trawler and alongside *Liberator*, where they received prompt assistance from Percy and two of the crewmen.

Donovan stood on the foredeck, deliberating what to do about the seven fishing boats. Behind him the topside bridge, which had been designed in a teardrop shape with the broad end to the bow, reared not quite two stories high. As with the rest of the prototype nuclear submarine, the blister was completely hydrodynamic. The ladders leading to the deck and the splash rails even retracted when *Liberator* dived. Although the relatively low blister virtually ensured that anyone on top became drenched during rough seas, the hydrodynamic profile added an extra five knots to the speed the ship could attain while submerged.

"What happened over there, Captain?" Executive Officer Percy asked. "We saw the fight, but those Japanese appeared out of nowhere and our men couldn't fire without endangering your lives."

"More damn crazies," Donovan said.

"Should we sink the trawlers?"

Donovan pursed his lips thoughtfully. Initially *Liberator* had carried forty Mark 70 long-range, laser-guided, acoustic-homing torpedoes with a range of 25,000 yards. There were also two dozen

31

antiship missiles with a range of 250 miles. The blue-green lasers, which could be employed as a probe or as a weapon, could knock out enemy electrical systems and would be useless against the trawlers.

"It would be a piece of cake to send them to Davy Jones's locker, sir," Percy insisted.

"No," Donovan said, making his decision. "I want to save our torpedoes and missiles for when they'll really be needed. We've already expended three fish against *Nemesis*. We shouldn't waste any more."

Percy gestured at the fishing boat. "But what about the crazies on board?"

"They'll kill each other off or die of radiation poisoning, if that's what they have."

Alex stared at the trawlers, then at the broken video camera. "Do you plan to inspect the other boats?"

"It would be a waste of time."

"But what if there's a survivor on one of them who hasn't succumbed to the psychosis?"

"We'll hail each trawler before we depart. None of us speak Japanese, but if there's a normal survivor on any of those boats, odds are he'll come on deck to check us out."

"Unless the crazies have the survivors trapped below decks."

Donovan opened his mouth to respond when there came a beep from the transceiver clipped to Percy's belt and the executive officer whipped the device to his lips.

"Yes?"

"Contact, sir. Nine miles off the port bow," Dave Jennings reported. "It's *Nemesis*."

Donovan headed for the hatch on the double. "If there are any survivors on those fishing boats, they'll have to wait."

* * *

An atmosphere of tense expectancy gripped the bridge. Donovan could feel it, seated in his swivel chair behind Hooper, his eyes on the Cyclops display. The icon representing *Nemesis* lay exactly where he'd first seen it upon returning to the bridge from the trawler—nine miles out and holding.

"What can she be up to now, sir?" Percy asked. "All she's doing is sitting there, waiting."

"Maybe whoever is on her is just letting us know they're there," Donovan speculated. "Nothing else makes much sense."

"They're within torpedo range, Captain."

"True, but given the capability that they've demonstrated in the past, at this range they could easily evade our fish," Donovan said, and glanced at the communications officer. "Status, Mr. Jennings?"

"The same old story, Captain. *Nemesis* is at one thousand feet, the same as us. She's emitting on fourteen-twenty hertz, the same as before. I'm not getting any screw signature."

Donovan slumped in his chair and frowned. He debated lighting a Lucky Strike and reflected on the bizarre behavior exhibited by their "twin." What the hell were those jokers trying to prove? Why were they baiting *Liberator* again and again and again? His mounting frustration seethed near the breaking point.

"Captain, the emissions have changed again and gone to fifteen hundred hertz," Jennings reported.

"And we know what that means," Donovan muttered.

"Nemesis is moving. She's diving."

"Let me know when she's at two thousand feet."

"Aye, Captain."

From his position behind the swivel chair, Charlie spoke up. "There was no rhyme or reason to that maneuver, Tom."

33

"It's a war of nerves. They're trying to wear us down, then close in for the kill," Donovan guessed.

"Or they're trying to catch us napping, sir," Percy interjected.

Sullenly, Donovan watched the *Nemesis* dive deeper, the icon dwindling on the viewscreen.

"Target is at two thousand feet," Jennings reported.

"Okay. Track her as long as you can," Donovan instructed. "Mr. Hooper, take us to the surface and resume our original heading. Ahead one-half. I want to be at the Marshall Islands by this evening."

"Aye, Captain," the youthful helmsman responded.

Alex, who had been standing next to Charlie during the ten-minute standoff, coughed lightly. "And those fishing boats?"

"They're on their own," Donovan replied. "We can't risk taking the time to board all of those trawlers with *Nemesis* prowling about. We'd be sitting ducks."

Clearly displeased by the decision, Alex simply nodded and exited the bridge.

"What's eating her?" Charlie wondered.

Donovan shrugged. "Mr. Percy, you have the bridge. Cancel alert stations."

"Yes, sir."

Walking leisurely forward, conveying an attitude of nonchalance, Donovan waited until he was out of sight of anyone on the bridge and then hastened after her. In thirty seconds he spied her lithe form up ahead and hurried to catch up. "Alex! Wait."

She halted and turned, her eyes focal points of accusation, her features registering a hint of sadness. "I thought you were keeping watch for *Nemesis.*"

"Percy will inform me if she shows up again. I

34

want to know what's bothering you. Why are you so insistent on checking those Japanese fishing boats? I would if I could. You know that."

"I know," Alex said, and sighed. "It's just that I can't help thinking about what would have happened to me, and everyone else in San Francisco, if you hadn't arrived when you did. The white-shirts would have burned us or that bastard Barbarosa would have fed us to the wolves by now."

Donovan took her hand in his. *"Liberator* came to San Francisco in the proverbial nick of time," he agreed. "What does that have to do with the trawlers?"

"I'm alive because you were there when I needed you. Now we have the opportunity to do the same for others, and it upsets me that we're leaving without verifying whether there are survivors on those boats. We might be their only hope and we're abandoning them."

"It can't be helped."

"I know, but the knowledge doesn't make the reality any more palatable."

Donovan gave her right shoulder a gentle squeeze. "I'm afraid we'll be forced to make a lot of hard decisions in the weeks and months ahead. We won't always like what we have to do, but we'll have to do it anyway."

Alex grinned. "A man does what a man has to do, huh?"

"Something like that."

A newcomer suddenly intruded on their conversation in a tone laced with sarcasm. "Well, well, well. Ain't this real cozy?"

"Hello, Lisa," Donovan said, recognizing the voice. He faced the black-haired teenager they had brought aboard at San Francisco along with a skinny kid named Jake. They had both been members of Barbarosa's Legion. Their former leader, a fundamentalist who developed delusions of grandeur and mistakenly believed he should rule the Earth, had been slain in a grisly, appropriate fashion. "Where's Jake?"

"The geek is in the mess feedin' his face," Lisa responded. "What a loser."

"Don't you like him?"

"What's to like? He's just a kid."

Donovan suppressed an impulse to laugh. Lisa and Jake were both the same age, sixteen. They had been devoted followers of Barbarosa, but that fanaticism had faded with time. Both had been injured during the final battle for San Francisco, Jake with a bullet crease to the temple and Lisa with a superficial wound in the abdomen. They both had recovered quickly, and although Peter Fisher wanted Lisa to stay in the sick bay for another few days, she obstinately refused and had been making a prime nuisance of herself.

"I thought the two of you were friends," he said.

"He's a dork," Lisa stated, and slid her hands in her jeans. She also wore a brown blouse and a faded, torn, black leather jacket that she had scrounged in San Francisco and refused to part with for anyone.

"How's your stomach?" Alex inquired.

"It's comin' along," Lisa replied, and nodded at Donovan. "No thanks to your boyfriend."

"Don't blame me. You were trying to kill us when I shot you," Donovan stated. "Be thankful I'm not a marksman like my brother, or you wouldn't be with us right now."

"I wish I wasn't. Why the hell did you bring me along, anyway? I didn't want to come."

"You required proper medical attention. We didn't want your wound to become infected."

"Who's this 'we'?"

"Dr. Fisher and myself."

36

Lisa looked at Alex. "Your brother has been pokin' and proddin' me ever since I stepped on this tub. He's been givin' me all kinds of tests, too. What does it all mean?"

"Why don't you ask him?"

"I did. But the son of a bitch won't tell me diddly."

"I don't know, either," Alex said.

"Sure," Lisa stated, managing to convey a complete lack of conviction. "Sure you don't."

"Is there anything we can do for you?" Donovan offered.

"Yeah. You can tell me where Hooper is."

"Helmsman Dave Hooper?"

Lisa snorted. "You know any other Hoopers on this tub, twinkletoes?"

"No," Donovan admitted. "Hooper is on duty at the moment. He'll be relieved in several hours."

"Good." Lisa abruptly wheeled and walked toward the bow.

"Now what was that all about?" Donovan asked.

"I saw Hooper and her talking in the mess last night," Alex mentioned. "I think they're hitting it off."

"I'd better have a talk with Hooper. She's just a kid."

"She's sixteen, Tom. Old enough to make her own decisions about personal relationships. The old rules don't apply anymore. Society's taboos crumbled when society collapsed."

"I brought her on board. I feel a certain responsibility toward her."

"You're not her father."

"Have you talked with her? Do you know much about her past?"

Alex shook her head. "She's a tight-lipped little hussy. I've tried to be friendly, but I can't get her to open up," she said, and laughed.

"What's so funny?"

"I can remember when you thought *I* had an attitude problem."

Donovan had to chuckle. "Yeah. She makes you look like Little Bo Peep in comparison." He stood stock-still for a moment, his senses in tune with the subtle motions of the submarine. "We're surfacing. Why don't we go topside?"

"I'd love to, but I promised Peter I'd help him on the computers," Alex replied. She glanced both ways, ensuring they were temporarily alone, and pecked him on the cheek. "Naval decorum and all that," she quipped, and headed for the sick bay.

Donovan watched her go, feeling slightly amazed that such an attractive, caring woman happened to be head over heels in love with him. He'd never been much of a ladies' man, which made her affection all the more mystifying. Oh, he'd known a few women intimately over the years, but his first love had always been the sea and his career. Few women were able to tolerate the prolonged absences the life of a seaman entailed, and most of his relationships had broken apart because of that fact.

Shaking his head to clear his thoughts, Donovan returned to the bridge to find everything in order. Jennings reported that there had been no further trace of *Nemesis.* Hooper informed him they were cruising on the surface at half-speed, already a mile from the Japanese fishing fleet. And Executive Officer Percy related their position as ninety nautical miles northeast of the Marshall Islands. Satisfied with the ship's status, Donovan ventured onto the topside bridge with Charlie and Percy.

A spray of salt water sprinkled Donovan's face as he stared to the southwest, wondering what they would find in Micronesia. The South Pacific islands promised to be their safest haven from the ravages

38

of the war, and he looked forward to establishing a base of operations there.

"I've fed what little information we had on those fishing boats into the Cray," Percy mentioned. "I'm hoping we can get a fix on where they were when all hell broke loose."

"Wherever they were, the firestorms missed them," Charlie remarked.

"Let's hope the firestorms missed the Marshall Islands," Donovan said.

A school of dolphins passed by off the port side, twenty or more, their graceful forms streaking clear of the water in powerful leaps. The adults were eight and a half feet in length with brownish black sides and cream-colored bellies.

Donovan watched the dolphins frolic for a while, then inadvertently tensed when he spotted a distinctive dorsal fin cutting the waves a hundred yards beyond them.

"Do you see that shark?" Charlie asked idly.

"I see it," Donovan said, his skin crawling. He'd never been very fond of sharks, and his dislike had changed to outright loathing when a close friend had lost a leg to a thresher shark while surfing near San Clemente. The friend, Bob Mathews, had grown up in the same neighborhood in New York City and later traveled to southern California to make his fortune in real estate. Mathews had done quite well, acquiring a two-million-dollar home, a fun-loving wife, and two bouncy kids. Every Sunday, rain or shine, he had gone to the beach to indulge his passion for surfing. Ten years ago, at the age of twenty-seven, in the prime of his life, Mathews went into the surf, paddled his board out, and was about to catch a wave when the shark took hold of his left leg. He'd gone under several times, screaming for help whenever he broke the surface, and finally the shark let him go. But most of his leg went with the shark. Other surfers rescued him, and he survived to continue in real estate, but he was never quite the same man after that. Some of his zest for life disappeared. Donovan had visited him on several occasions, and every time he thought of Mathews's stump he got a bad case of the willies.

The miles went by swifly. Two. Four. Five.

Donovan glanced back, reflecting on the poor souls on the seven trawlers, experiencing a twinge of regret that he hadn't done more to verify there were no survivors on the boats. Just as he looked, to his utter astonishment, the northern horizon blazed with the fiery, mushrooming brilliance of a nuclear detonation.

5

Captain First Rank Ivan Vazov dreamed of happier times.

He dreamed of his wife, Ludmila, of her soft brown hair and her fascinating brown eyes, eyes that could miraculously convey to him all the love in the world. He dreamed of his two sons, Iosif and Vsevolod, and the joy he had felt when they were small boys and he could bounce them on his knee, letting them pretend they were riding a bucking bronc like those cowboys in the American Westerns. He dreamed of those tranquil days when he would take the boys to Gorki Park in Moscow and watch them sail their toy boats on the pond. For minutes he drifted in a state of semiconsciousness, vividly recalling the happiest moments of his life, on the verge of waking up but dreading the prospect of opening his eyes. Only when the intercom in his cabin blared did he reluctantly rouse himself to full awareness.

"Captain Vazov to the control room! Captain Vazov to the control room!"

Startled, Vazov rose and tugged on his cabin door. He recognized the voice as belonging to Dragominov, and he wondered what could possibly have gotten ten the normally reserved executive officer so agitated. From his cabin, which was one of sixteen such comfortable compartments located aft, he hurried along the narrow corridors, past the engine room and the reactor, to the control room. The second his stocky frame appeared in the doorway all eyes turned toward him and he knew, with a dreadful certainty, that the moment of truth was upon them all.

"Captain Vazov!" Nikolai Dragominov exclaimed in obvious relief. He stood near the crewman manning the communications console.

Vazov nodded and walked forward, forcing himself to reflect a calm demeanor, to put on a composed front for the benefit of his men. "Report, Nikolai."

"A nuclear detonation, Comrade Captain. Range, twenty miles. Bearing one-seven-zero," Dragominov stated, nearly bubbling over in his excitement.

The blood seemed to suddenly rush to Vazov's temples and his heart seemed to beat faster, pounding in his barrel of a chest. He inhaled slowly so his surging adrenaline could subside. "A nuclear detonation? You are sure?"

"Yes, Comrade Captain," the lieutenant verified. "The readings have been triple-checked. The yield is estimated at five kilotons or under."

"So small?" Vazov said, and scratched his square chin. "A ship-to-ship missile, perhaps."

"That would be my guess, Comrade Captain."

Vazov became intensely aware of the looks of the crew. Each one was waiting for him to make the decision that would set them on a course to fulfill the mission for which they had been created. The weariness pervading his being, the uncharacteristic lethargy he had felt for weeks, made him want to curl up on his bunk, pull a blanket over his head, and forget the world existed. But as the commander of one of the finest subs in the Soviet navy, as a man who had spent decades faithfully performing his duty, he addressed them with his customary air of rigid authority. "Battle stations, Comrade Dragominov."

"Yes, sir!" the executive officer responded enthusiastically, and sounded the alarm.

Vazov glanced at his helmsman, Ivachko Kuprevici. "Status, Ivachko?"

"The hull indicator lights are all green, Captain. We are cleared to dive."

"Then dive," Vazov ordered. "Flood the main ballast tanks and take her down at ten degrees."

"Diving, Captain."

The red lights in the control room dimmed as the nuclear-powered submarine began her slow descent. All hands were engrossed at their duty stations, their eyes riveted to monitors and gauges.

And so it begins! Vazov thought. He placed his hands on his hips and kept a watchful gaze on his men, all seasoned crewmen with the exception of young Dragominov, whose meteoric rise through the ranks, some said, could be attributed more to his father's political influence than his competence. But those who made such accusations did not know Dragominov very well, for in the six months that the junior officer had sailed under him, Vazov had learned to respect Dragominov's expertise and brilliance. Besides, as any idiot should know, only the very best were assigned to the *Charkov.*

The cream of the Soviet crop of nuclear subs, the *Charkov* had made her maiden run only a year before the war. Her technology was the best copy of American achievements that rubles could buy. Or steal. Thousands of KGB man-hours had been spent obtaining highly classified American documents so that Soviet scientists and engineers could study them and adopt the schematics to the needs of the Soviet navy. The propulsion system on the *Charkov* was a virtual replica of the latest nuclear reactors in use on American subs. Her hull had been

43

streamlined along the lines of the Los Angeles class of nuclear vessels. And her size, in keeping with a long-standing Soviet tradition of building ships that were larger, if not better, than their American counterparts, was gargantuan. Five hundred feet in length, with a conning tower that rose three stories above the upper deck, the *Charkov* resembled nothing else so much as a great gray shark.

The *Charkov* dwarfed the previous biggest subs, the Typhoon-class juggernauts first put in service in 1980. Both types of craft shared similar characteristics. Both were heavier than a pocket battleship—the Typhoon class at 25,000 tons and the *Charkov* at 30,000 tons. Both contained enormous ballast tanks, and both were twin-hulled as an added protection against sinking when hit by an ememy torpedo or missile. Each type of submarine was powered by two nuclear reactors, which in turn provided the steam for two sets of turbines that drove twin five-bladed propellers. But the *Charkov* could attain speeds and depths unreachable by the Typhoon-class ships. Thanks to significant improvements in the reactor design and the turbines, the *Charkov* had reached sixty knots on her trial runs.

Perhaps the most significant difference lay in the weaponry. While the Typhoon-class submarines could boast twenty launch tubes and carried thirty SS-N-22 Seawind missiles and thirty Spearfish torpedoes as their standard armament immediately preceding the war, the *Charkov* carried forty Seawind missiles and forty Tigerfish torpedoes. The latter were the equal of any of the Americans could muster and had a maximum range of 23,000 meters.

Then there was the SHADOW stalking system and its component veiling unit. Developed only four months prior to the outbreak of hostilities, the

SHADOW incorporated the ship's sonar, computers, and diverse automation systems into a centralized tracking and maneuvering program. In essence, the Leonid-5 computer, the central core or "brain" of the system, enabled the *Charkov* to home in on any vessel and to stalk that ship, to duplicate every maneuver made by the enemy while slowly approaching from the rear.

The heart of the SHADOW was the Vostoy, a revolutionary shrouding device that totally concealed the *Charkov* from detection by enemy sonar or similar systems. In conjunction with the automated SHADOW, the Vostoy rendered the *Charkov* virtually invisible. During test runs in the Baltic Sea and the North Pacific, the *Charkov* had successfully shadowed surface and submerged craft, consistently approaching to within one hundred meters without being discovered. A few sonar operators on the target vessels had reported intermittent, vague echoes, but that was all.

"Take us down to two hundred meters," Vazov said.

If the *Charkov* possessed any weakness, it lay in the sub's diving and surfacing capabilities. Due to its immense bulk, the *Charkov* could attain only two-thirds of the speed that American subs could reach when diving. But while on the surface or once submerged, the *Charkov* could match them tit for tat.

"Passing fifty meters," Dragominov announced.

"Level off at two hundred," Vazov commanded, then stiffened when a low voice called out from behind him.

"Our hour of glory is upon us, Comrades!"

His features set in stone, Vazov turned and acknowledged the presence of Captain Second Rank Serge Vatutin, the *Charkov*'s political officer.

A bulldog of a man whose perpetually shifting

eyes gave him an appropriately devious appearance, Serge Vatutin had been assigned to the *Charkov* because his devotion to the Motherland bordered on the fanatical. His daily pep talks to the crew were delivered with the passion of a religious zealot. To serve the Motherland was everything. Nothing else mattered. And anyone who displayed the slightest trace of dissatisfaction would come under Vatutin's close scrutiny.

Vazov despised the man.

"Have we made contact with the *Liberator?*" Vatutin asked hopefully. "Has our moment of retribution finally arrived?"

"Our sensors have detected a nuclear detonation twenty miles away. We are en route to investigate," Vazov said.

"The *Liberator?*"

"We have no way of knowing yet," Vazov responded patiently.

"Let us hope it is the accursed Americans," Vatutin stated harshly. "We will finally have our revenge for the obliteration of our Motherland."

"We don't know that the Motherland has been obliterated," Vazov mentioned. "Certainly, whole cities have been devastated, but—"

"How can you stand there and discuss the ruin of Mother Russia so clinically?" the political officer asked, aghast. "Every man on board has lost those he loves the most. Our beloved country has been reduced to ashes. Millions upon millions have perished." He paused, his dark eyes wide and unfocused. "We have a responsibility to the Motherland to seek out and eradicate every enemy ship we can find! We have a responsibility to our families to see that they lie peacefully in their graves, knowing their lives have been avenged."

Vazov bristled and took a half step forward. "Don't tell *me* about responsibility! I know what my duties are and I have discharged them faithfully."

Vatutin blinked a few times. "I did not mean to imply you were less than a loyal Party member—"

"If I wasn't loyal, the High Command wouldn't have assigned me to command the best attack sub in the fleet. It is our misfortune that we were conducting a test off the Arctic when the war started, depriving us of the opportunity to acquit ourselves with honor," Vazov said, thinking of the last orders the *Charkov* had received from the Northern Fleet High Command two days before the holocaust. "Proceed to the East Siberian Sea," the orders had read, "submerge to seven hundred meters, and maintain radio silence." Several antisubmarine frigates were supposed to have arrived in the area four days after the *Charkov* submerged to attempt to locate her using the latest in sub-detection technology. The whole purpose of the test had been to determine if the *Charkov* could elude detection. But the frigates had never shown up. Knowing the crafty nature of the practice drills set up by the High Command, Vazov had remained submerged for a week, suspecting that the frigates might be lying back, waiting for his curiosity to get the better of him and compel him to commit a blunder by surfacing prematurely. By the time he did venture to the surface, the war was over.

And yet it wasn't over.

There were bound to be American vessels that had survived. The United States had had forty-five nuclear-powered ballistic submarines in operation at the outset of World War Three, and Vazov found it difficult to believe that all of them had been eliminated. And several weeks ago, while cruising through the Bering Sea, they had picked up a faint radio report from a pilot who identified himself as Ari Fessenkov and who claimed to be flying an old

47

Mikoyan-Gurevich 15, a MIG-15, used in the Korean War. Fessenkov rambled on about strafing an American submarine, and the description he gave of the ship had aroused Vazov's interest to a fever pitch. Vazov had tried to contact the pilot, to no avail. After thirty minutes the transmission had ended. Because the signals were so weak, Communications had been unable to triangulate Fessenkov's exact location.

Although Fessenkov had blabbered incoherently during his transmissions, and even though the enemy sub's position was unknown, Vazov had decided to hunt for the American sub on the off chance that Fessenkov had been telling the truth. The description the old pilot had given matched precisely with the known contours of the U.S.S. *Liberator*, the newest and perhaps ultimate projection of American sea power. Soviet Naval Intelligence had alerted all subs in the Northern Fleet to be on the lookout for the *Liberator* over six weeks ago, back when there still was a Soviet naval apparatus in operation.

The thought troubled Vazov. He'd been unprepared for the total devastation they'd found as the *Charkov* sailed from the East Siberian Sea, through the Gulf of Anadyr, and into the Bering Sea. Staying close to the coast, they had stopped at every port along the way. Everywhere, they found the same horror. Blistered buildings, a scorched landscape, and demented looters who would attack the crew on sight. They had lost two seamen at Anadyr when a mob of insane survivors, many of whom were dressed in white shirts, ambushed a landing party.

The loss of the two seamen prompted Vazov to realize he must keep his crew on board until the situation on land had improved. He couldn't afford to lose another crew member. With fourteen officers

48

and one hundred and ten seamen, the *Charkov* had barely enough personnel to man all duty stations twenty-four hours a day. His men were under enough strain without the added burden of extra duty hours.

Aware that his mind had strayed yet again, a disturbing tendency he had developed in recent days, Vazov focused on Serge Vatutin's ugly countenance and caught the last half of the political officer's response.

"—granted us another chance to die with honor, if need be. The *Liberator* is out there somewhere. All we need to do is find her."

"And we will," Vazov vowed. "We will pay them back for the deaths of our families. Who knows how many of our cities this *Liberator* laid waste to with her missiles? We will investigate the nuclear explosion, and if the *Liberator* is involved, we will track her and send her to a watery grave."

6

At 1130 hours, ten miles southwest of where the Japanese fishing fleet had been vaporized, *Liberator* knifed through the Pacific at half speed, submerged at a depth of one thousand feet.

"Ahead full, Mr. Hooper," Donovan ordered, shifting in his chair, and studied the Cyclops display. Nothing. Not a trace of *Nemesis*. He had taken the ship down immediately after the blast and waited for their phantom twin to put in an appearance, but the wait had been fruitless. "Resume our original heading to the Marshall Islands."

"Aye, Captain."

Donovan glanced over his left shoulder at Charlie, Alex, and Peter, who had gathered on the bridge and listened expectantly while Sensors swept the sea for any indication of their elusive adversary and readings were taken of the blast area. He tried to inject a lighthearted tone into his voice. "Well, that's all the entertainment for today."

"Sort of a dull show," Charlie quipped. "We didn't even get any popcorn."

"I should be returning to sick bay," Peter announced, and departed.

Alex, a peculiar expression on her face, her eyes absently roving over the screen, asked, "Why?"

"Who the hell knows?" Donovan said bitterly.

50

"I mean, why would *Nemesis* bother to destroy a puny fleet of harmless trawlers? What purpose did it serve?"

"If you want my opinion," Charlie said, "for what it's worth I think they were sending us a message, showing off their stuff and letting us know that they can take us down anytime they want to."

"Can they?"

"No," Donovan declared. "Our sensors would detect any incoming missiles or torpedoes they fired at us and we would take the necessary evasive actions."

"But your sensors didn't detect the missile they fired at the fishing fleet," Alex noted.

"True, but the trawlers were between *Nemesis* and us. They used the fishing boats as a screen. The warhead they fired was small, similar to the field-grade warhead in the Mark 97N we used on the bus terminal in San Francisco."

"Maybe they fired a surface skimmer," Charlie suggested.

"A what?" Alex inquired.

"Both sides were working on perfecting surface-skimming missiles during the late nineties and after the turn of the century," Donovan answered. "The idea was to have a missile fly toward a target at a height of ten or twenty feet above the surface, which would make getting a radar fix extremely difficult. Neither side developed a workable system, though, because of all the kinks that remained to be worked out. For one thing, the engineers weren't able to overcome the problem of the missile maintaining a steady lock on the target at such a low elevation. That's why missiles normally follow a curved trajectory." He paused. "Even cruise missiles, which can descend and skim the surface of the ocean below a warship's radar horizon, have to be launched outside the range of an enemy's radar and then swoop down to close in."

"The British used a sea-skimming missile regularly years ago," Charlie mentioned. "The Sea Skua was launched from a helicopter against patrol boats. They never used them in ship-to-ship warfare, though."

Alex sighed and placed her hands on the top of the chair. "Nuclear warheads. Cruise missiles. Torpedoes. I know next to nothing about the technology used in our instruments of war, and I find it all more than just a little frightening."

"The operating principles are easy to comprehend," Donovan said.

"That's easy for you to say," Alex responded. "The Navy has been your life."

"I'll give you an example. A cruise missile, once it's airborne, is guided by the information that was fed into its computer before its launch. Once the missile gets within radar range of its target, the radar seeker activates and locks on to the enemy. That's when the battle of wits ensues between the missile and the target's electronic jamming techniques," Donovan detailed.

"So you're saying that if *Nemesis* fires a missile at us, *Liberator*'s sensors would pick it up and we would try to jam the missile?"

"Exactly."

"And our sensors would always detect an incoming missile?"

"Unless we were *really* careless."

"Thanks. Now I feel a lot better," Alex said dryly.

Donovan regarded her for a moment. "This isn't quite what you expected, is it?"

"I can't complain. When you offered me the job of scientist aboard *Liberator,* I envisioned a golden opportunity to do research in a first-class lab. I saw a chance to tour the world, and at the same time

I'd be helping to cure ills. But I didn't fully realize that the war isn't over."

"It ain't over until the fat lady sings," Charlie cracked, and when Alex gave him a cold stare he shrugged and grinned. "I heard that somewhere once."

"I'm sorry," Donovan apologized. "I should have explained the situation in greater detail. No, the war isn't over. Besides *Nemesis*, we must keep a watch for any Soviet vessels that weren't destroyed. Their navy was larger than ours, so the odds that a few of their warships are still around are very good."

"I'll say their navy was larger," Charlie said. "The Russians had sixty-two nuclear-powered ballistic-missile subs in commission, fifty guided-missile subs, and twenty conventional subs. We're bound to run into one of them sooner or later."

"And when we do?" Alex asked.

"We can't take any chances," Donovan said. "If they hail us and announce their peaceful intentions, we'll arrange a truce. But otherwise, we'll fire first and experience regrets later."

"Excuse me, Captain," Executive Officer Percy interjected, coming over. "I couldn't help but overhear. Do you still have doubts that the Soviets started the war?"

"We have no concrete proof that they did."

"Who else would have had the motive?" Percy queried. "The hard-liners had regained control of the Kremlin and kicked the liberal premier out on his can. They were pushing us, weren't they? How many protests had we lodged against them for intruding into our territory or flying into our air space? How many deliberate rammings by Soviet vessels had been reported by our skippers while our boys were on maneuvers in the open seas? Dozens."

"You have a valid point," Donovan conceded.

"But the Soviets weren't crazy. They knew they had everything to lose by starting a nuclear war. Our administration would have given them concessions at the bargaining table, and they knew it. The whole purpose of the conference was to work out an agreement with the Russians. Nobody in the West wanted a conflict."

Charlie listened attentively to the argument. He knew all about the conference because he'd been assigned to protect the restricted area when *Nemesis* shot him down. The president, the defense ministers of Japan, and representatives from the Peoples Republic of China and the newly reunited Germany had all gathered on a carrier in the Sea of Japan to discuss their strategies for coexisting peacefully with the Russians.

"Maybe the Russians thought they could launch a preemptive strike and get away with it," Percy speculated. "Maybe they thought they would paralyze our military establishment by taking out the president and his staff."

"Maybe," Donovan said, "but until we uncover conclusive evidence, I'll view the issue with an open mind."

Percy shook his head and moved away.

"There goes a man ready to stomp Russian butt," Charlie remarked.

"Hopefully, we won't have to," Donovan said.

Alex stared at the man she loved, perplexed by his statement. "I thought warfare was your stock in trade. Part of it, anyway."

"And part of it is," Donovan stated. "But the world has seen enough violence to last a millennium. When future generations look at World War Three in retrospect, I think they'll view it as a testimony to humanity's ultimate stupidity. There has been enough fighting," he stressed, and gazed into her eyes. "What the world needs now is to be rebuilt from the ground up, and we're in a prime position to do something about that, to contribute in a meaningful way. Conflicts with the Soviets would only divert us from our goal and might even end our mission completely."

"Then let's hope we don't run into any Russians," Alex said.

"Only time will tell."

The setting sun had transformed the western horizon into a dazzling display of vivid red, yellow, and orange shades when *Liberator* broke the surface and Donovan climbed to the topside bridge. Executive Officer Percy, Systems Chief Smith, Communications Officer Jennings, and several other officers joined him. Helmsman Hooper handled the wheel.

"We should arrive at the Marshall Islands in three hours," Donovan informed them. "I've called this meeting to get your input on our strategy once we're there."

"We've already agreed that locating a safe base of operations is essential," Chief Smith said. "And while I would have preferred to establish our base in the States, our run-ins with the white-shirts in San Francisco and elsewhere have shown me that the idea is impractical."

"Why are we starting our search in the Marshall Islands? I thought we were going to begin looking in the Society Islands," Percy observed.

"Initially we were," Donovan said. "But Alex ran a study on the Cray-9. Her projections indicate we have a good chance of finding the ideal island in the Marshalls. And since the Marshall Islands have been governed by the United States as part of the United Nations Trust Territory of the Pacific Islands, no one can dispute our legal claim to whichever island we decide to take over."

"Begging your pardon, sir," Percy said, "but who could possibly dispute our claim, whether it's legal or not?"

"Probably no one," Donovan admitted. "Still, we are a Navy unit and we'll do everything by the book. Is that understood?"

"Aye, Captain," Percy responded.

"How big are the Marshalls?" Jennings inquired.

"They have an area of around seventy square miles and a coastline of about eighty. Altogether, there are thirty-four islands and coral atolls, and eleven hundred and fifty islets. The Marshalls lie in two parallel chains situated about a hundred and thirty miles apart. We'll commence our sweep along the eastern chain, or Radak, as it's called."

"What about the natives?" Chief Smith asked. "Are we going to boot them out?"

"No. We'll do our utmost to establish peaceful relations with the indigenous population, if there is anyone left. We can't predict how the firestorms might have affected the Marshalls because we're still not clear on exactly how many firestorms there were, what their duration might have been, and, most important, their intensity."

"After Seattle, we have a fair idea of their intensity," Chief Smith commented.

Donovan gazed at the splendid sunset, the warm air caressing his cheeks. "On the plus side, the climate in the Marhsalls is tropical. We won't need to worry about frigid winters. The computer tells us that rainfall on the southernmost islands is rather heavy, but the precipitation is light on the northern ones. Breadfruit trees and coconut palms grow in abundance, and there are plenty of fish among the reefs. We won't starve, either."

"It sounds like Paradise," Percy said.

"On the negative side, I'm concerned about the

possibility of earthquakes and possibly volcanoes," Donovan informed them.

"Earthquakes in the Marshalls?" Chief Smith queried.

"Not specifically, but the area south of the Marshalls, the area between New Zealand, Tonga, and New Guinea, is the most active earthquake zone in the world. We already know that the nuclear explosions triggered seismic activity in the vicinity of San Francisco. It's anyone's guess what might have happened in the South Pacific."

"We haven't recorded any seismicity en route," Jennings noted. "The East Pacific Rise, the Murray Fracture Zone, and the Clarion Fracture Zone were all quiet."

"Let's hope the sea floor stays quiet," Donovan said.

"The sooner we locate a safe base, the better," Chief Smith remarked. "We've had to postpone some regularly scheduled minor maintenance on the reactor because we haven't sat still long enough to get the job done."

The mention of the reactor made Donovan think of *Liberator*'s propulsion system, the finest in the world. A Westinghouse NCS Superfluid Metal Coolant Reactor took up the portion of the sub just aft of amidships and forward of the engine room. The basic design for the reactor stemmed from the model used flawlessly for a decade at the Fermi National Laboratory in Batavia, Illinois. The engineers were able to eliminate the primary coolant pump by using superfluid dibarium as a coolant in the convection design, thereby eliminating one of the major sources of noise in a nuclear submarine. The reactor core had a projected life span of thirty years and could run indefinitely on the fuel it already had.

In the engine room were three T7W steam turbines built especially for *Liberator* by General Dynamics. One was always kept off-line as a spare while the other two were in use. The power plant was currently performing at peak efficiency and had posed no problems since the ship had been put in service.

Thanks to the efficiency of the heat-transfer mechanism on the nuclear-steam link, the NCS reactor and T7W turbines could easily propel *Liberator* at up to sixty knots—perhaps even higher, but she had never been put through the wringer to determine her maximum speed.

"You'll get the time you need soon," Donovan promised. "Once we locate a suitable base, you'll have all the time in the world."

"Sensors need to have maintenance performed, too," Communications Officer Jennings stated.

"Why do you say that?" Donovan asked.

"Because the system has developed a minor glitch. Three times we've registered a weak contact at varying ranges, and each time I've triple-checked immediately with active sonar and our other systems. Each check showed nothing there."

Donovan tensed. "Are you sure it's a glitch? Could it be *Nemesis?*"

"No, Captain. I'm sure of it. All I'm getting is a fuzzy ghost image, so faint the sensors barely register, every now and then. It's a minor malfunction, nothing more."

"Will it impair the ability of the sensors to recognize a legitimate target?"

"No, sir."

"Then we won't worry about the glitch right now. The night shift systems-repair crew can look for it," Donovan said, and stretched. "Once we arrive in the Marshalls, we'll lay off the first island we find, get a good night's sleep, and venture into Paradise in the morning."

"Sometimes these glitches are hard to track down, sir," Jennings remarked.

"If they find it, they find it. Right now a fuzzy false contact is the least of our worries."

7

The crew of *Liberator* began their search for a safe haven the next morning at 0630. Executive Officer Percy stood on the topside bridge along with Helmsman Hooper and watched a party of four head toward the first land any of them had seen in a week, an atoll. The ring-shaped coral island, open to the east, enclosed a shallow lagoon.

Donovan, Alex, Charlie, and Chief Smith comprised the landing party, with the latter handling the chore of operating the small outboard that powered their raft. The three men took along Franchis—"Just in case," as Charlie put it.

"It's beautiful," Alex breathed, admiring the striking hues accented by the rising sun.

Donovan simply nodded, thinking of the restless night he'd experienced, all that tossing and turning and fidgeting, despite his best efforts to grab some shut-eye. Alex had slept soundly beside him, and he had spent many a minute stroking her silken hair in the darkness, annoyed at himself for not sleeping and unable to determine the reason why. Was it the excitement generated by the prospect of possibly being on the verge of securing a base of operations? Or was there another reason, one his subconscious recognized but his conscious mind didn't?

He'd roused out of the sack at 0530, taken a lei-surely shower, eaten heartily in the mess, then re-ported to the bridge to relieve the lieutenant who had been in charge of the night shift. Nothing un-usual had occurred overnight. The graveyard re-pair crew had conducted a thorough systems check on the sensors and failed to find any gremlins, which should have relieved Donovan but, strangely, left him with a gnawing, vague feeling of unease. He chalked his groundless jitters up to a case of bad nerves due to the repeated run-ins with *Nemesis*.

His first glimpse of the atoll through the peri-scope had sufficed to convince him that the island would not make an adequate base. He wanted a site adjacent to a natural deep-water port, a feature this atoll lacked. A port was necessary so *Liberator* could come and go undetected, a necessity considering that *Nemesis* waited somewhere out at sea to pounce whenever *Liberator* showed herself. Al-though the atoll did not pass muster, he wanted to step ashore to become acquainted with the flora and fauna proliferating in the Marshalls. That, and the fact he simply desired to tread firm land again after seven days at sea.

"There aren't any signs of natives," Charlie com-mented while scanning the lagoon. "No huts, no boats, no smoke."

"Good," Donovan said. The last thing he needed was a confrontation with unfriendly natives. Talk about a lousy way to start the day.

"This atoll is fairly typical of the Marshalls," Alex said. She spied a grove of coconut palm thirty yards to the south of the lagoon. "There might not be natives here now, but they were here once."

"How do you know?" Donovan inquired.

"Those coconut palms. They didn't develop as part of the evolutionary scheme in these islands. They were imported by man, and wherever they're

61

found, you can be sure they were planted by some-one."

"Is there any record of how many of the Marshall Islands and atolls are inhabited?" Chief Smith que-ried. "Or were inhabited, anyway."

"Our computer records indicate the great majority were inhabited before the war. Now, it's anyone's guess," Alex answered. "The exact population figure was seventy thousand, two hundred and seventy-one inhabitants."

"Then these islands must be crawling with na-tives," Charlie said.

"Not really. The total area of the archipelago is about seventy square miles," Alex informed them.

Donovan listened absently to the conversation, adrift in his own thoughts. The Cray-9 did not con-tain a list of the name for every island, atoll, and islet in the Marshalls, which led him to believe that some of them didn't even have official names. All he knew about the atoll they were almost upon was the location, 13 degrees north latitude and 170 de-grees east longitude, at the very northeast tip of the Marshalls and not far from Bikar Atoll, one of the more prominent ones in the whole chain.

"Hey. Pigeons," Alex declared, delighted at the initial sign of life, watching a small flock wing its way from south to north over the atoll.

"There are a lot of nonoceanic birds scattered throughout the islands," Alex disclosed. "But very few mammals."

"Too bad," Alex said. "I wouldn't mind sinking my teeth into some roast wild pig."

Chief Smith adroitly negotiated their raft through the reefs fringing the lagoon, then in-creased speed once they were in the open. The wa-ter became clearer, enabling them to observe the coarse coral sand at the bottom, fifteen feet under-neath the raft. A third of the distance across the lagoon the depth drastically increased, lost in the blue haze below. A variety of fish swam lazily to and fro, unruffled by the vibrations produced by the outboard.

A protracted sigh escaped Charlie's lips. "It figures this island would be uninhabited. I was hoping for a welcoming committee of lovely native women in skimpy skirts."

"I see a parrot," Alex said, staring at a large green bird perched on a limb in a stunted tree.

"Damn. And I didn't bring a cracker," Charlie quipped.

More parrots appeared as the raft drew nearer to the shore, along with swifts, kingfishers, and, of all things, starlings.

Donovan grasped his Franchi as the raft slowed, then stepped onto the shore the instant the raft touched the sand. Charlie joined him, and together they pulled the raft above the water line. Alex and Chief Smith clambered out.

"Do we split up or stick together, big brother?" Charlie asked.

"We'll split up," Donovan directed. "Flaze and you can take the south half, Alex and I will go to the north. If you find any sign of human habitation, give a yell."

"You've got it," Charlie assured him, and with Chief Smith on his heels moved off.

Alex gazed at the vegetation, which was sparse close to the lagoon and denser in the interior, admiring the pristine scene. "You know, a setting like this could turn a gal into an incurable romantic."

"Try to keep your mind on our work," Donovan said with a grin.

"Party pooper. If that's the way you want to be, let's see how big this island is."

They entered the trees and shrubs, hiking to the

63

northeast, listening to the calls of myriad birds. Lizards occasionally skittered from their path.

"Did the Cray say anything about poisonous snakes in the Marshalls?" Donovan queried.

"There are none. Just as there aren't any amphibians."

"All this water and no amphibians? No frogs? No salamanders? No newts?"

"No. Why? Are you fond of newts?"

"You know what I'm fond of."

Alex voiced a very unladylike snicker. "Don't I, though."

As with most Micronesian islands, the vegetation on the atoll became more luxuriant as they hiked toward the center, where the groundwater invariably was freshest. They meandered among the trees, enjoying the eighty-degree weather and the mild Pacific breeze. Two hundred yards from the lagoon, as Donovan crossed over a low knoll, one of the few on the essentially flat island, he happened to glance down at the ground and froze when he saw the imprint of a naked human foot in the soft earth. His abrupt halt almost caused Alex to bump into him.

"Hey, what's the holdup?" she inquired.

"Take a look," Donovan stated, squatting to inspect the footprint.

"At wh—" Alex began, then gasped. "Uh-oh."

"I'm no tracker, but I'd say this appears to be fresh," Donovan said. He pressed his fingertips lightly on the soil within the print, then traced his fingers around the edges.

"The track is pointing due west."

Donovan rose and hefted the Franchi. "Let's see where it leads."

"What about Charlie and Flaze? Shouldn't we warn them?"

"Not yet. If there are natives on this island,

64

they'll hear us if we start shouting or firing shots and come to investigate. This could be a lone hunter or fisherman."

"You hope."

"Come on," Donovan said, and bore westward, his senses now on edge, his eyes darting from tree to tree, fully alert. From the knoll they traversed a flat stretch of grass and trees, then came to a field of uninterrupted sword grass. At the far side, just walking into another belt of trees, was their native. "Down," Donovan whispered, and they crouched.

Few of the native's features could be distinguished other than a broad back, light brown skin, and straight black hair. He wore a tattered pair of brown pants and held a thin spear in his left hand.

"He seems to be in a hurry," Alex whispered.

"Maybe he saw us at the lagoon."

"Or saw the sub."

"We have to trail him," Donovan said.

They waited until the islander was out of sight, then stood and hurried in pursuit, crossing the sword grass quickly to get out of the open. A surprising development awaited them at the treeline in the form of a narrow, barely discernible path.

Donovan stopped and frowned. This meant that the natives must visit the island fairly frequently, and that there might be more elsewhere on the atoll. He hesitated, torn between returning to the raft to signal Pirate or following the native. Curiosity compelled him to do the latter.

The island turned out to be slightly over three hundred yards from east to west. A wide strip of beach bordered the Pacific at the northwest corner, and drawn up on the sand were four outrigger canoes. Milling about the outriggers were nine South Pacific natives, many of whom were carrying spears. Most had adopted European- or American-style clothing, jeans or other pants being worn by

all the men except three. The trio wore cloth gar-
ments that were little more than loincloths.

Taking cover behind the boles of trees, Donovan
and Alex watched for five minutes. Forty yards separated them from the beach, too far for them to
overhear snatches of conversation, which was undoubtedly being conducted in one of the eight languages spoken in Micronesia. Alex had searched the
Cray-9 files for information on the languages when
she researched Oceania as a likely region in which
to base the submarine.

Her study had revealed that even by the primitive standards prevailing in the South Pacific, the
native cultures in the Marshall Islands were simple. The natives were profoundly dependent on the
sea for their sustenance. Because the islanders
spent most of their time catching fish, their mari-
time abilities had reached a high level. The natives
had developed map making for extended voyages
and could navigate by the sun and the stars. Their
fishing skills, including the use of their traditional
slender spears, were exceptional.

Now Alex watched living examples of the people
she had studied intensely and speculated on the
reason for their presence on the atoll. Were the natives there to hunt? Were they planning to fish the
waters off the shore? Or were they simply taking a
break from their daily routine?

A few feet to her right, Donovan studied the canoes and recounted the natives. Nine. If his calculations were correct, there should be three natives
missing, provided there had been three to each outrigger. Where could they be? he wondered.

Mere seconds later an answer was forthcoming.
The natives at the canoes uttered exclamations and
gestured to the south, and there, being prodded by
the spears of the last three natives, was Charlie.
His wrists were tied at the base of his spine, and

there appeared to be a dark bruise or welt on his forehead.

"Pirate!" Donovan exclaimed softly, and refrained from charging from cover only through sheer force of will. If he tried to intervene to rescue his brother, the natives might run Charlie through on general principles.

"Where's Chief Smith?" Alex whispered.

Donovan shrugged, his left side pressed against the smooth tree trunk. The three natives passed within thirty yards of his position on their way to rejoin their companions, but he held his fire. Charlie glanced toward the trees and Donovan almost jumped up and waved.

The other natives clustered around the captive, motioning and talking excitedly. One of them, a tall man whose sun-bronzed skin and muscular build testified to his hardy life outdoors, seemed to be the leader. This tall man, who wore black pants, barked commands to the others, and within a minute the outriggers were being pushed into the surf. Charlie had been deposited in the stern of one of the boats, and he sat glumly while the islanders put to sea.

"Let's haul ass," Donovan said, jogging to the south. "We've got to find Flaze and get back to *Liberator*. We'll overtake those natives in no time."

"How do we convince them to turn over Charlie when we catch them?" Alex asked, keeping pace on his left.

"We'll cross that bridge when we come to it."

They ran toward the point at which they had first laid eyes on Charlie and the trio, then tried to backtrack from there. In spots the soil proved soft enough to bear tracks, and they were able to make slow but steady progress.

Alex, intuitively reading Donovan's inner turmoil as readily as she would the pages of a book, offered consolation. "I doubt the natives will do anything to Charlie until after they reach their village. We have plenty of time to overtake them."

Donovan nodded once, when suddenly he stiffened and paled, his gaze alighting on the prone form of Chief Smith lying ten yards away, a crimson stain rimming Flaze's head.

8

His heart thudding in his chest, Donovan raced to the chief's side and knelt. "Flaze?" he said, then gently rolled the big man on his back. A six-inch gash had dented Smith's forehead and blood still seeped from the left corner. A quick inspection verified there were no other wounds. "The sons of bitches must have slugged him with a club or something and left him for dead."

"They must have used this," Alex stated. Her left shoe flicked out and nudged a stout section of broken tree limb, the size of a baseball bat, lying a yard from the chief. Its bark had been spattered with crimson stains.

"Bastards," Donovan snapped bitterly. "Here," he said, and gave her the Franchi. With great effort, his shoulders straining, he succeeded in raising the systems chief and supporting Smith under the arms.

"I can lend you a hand," Alex offered.

"For all we know there might be more natives on this island," Donovan said. "Keep your eyes peeled and I'll lug him to the lagoon." So saying, he shuffled to the east, and he had only covered fifty yards when he began to breathe heavily and grit his teeth. He'd known he was somewhat out of shape, what with all the sitting he did on board the ship and the limited time he could afford to devote to exercising in the workout room, but he'd had no idea how badly out of condition he was until that moment.

Alex, watching him grunt and turn red in the face, tried again. "Are you sure I can't help you?"

"I'm fine," Donovan gurgled.

"If you say so."

For Donovan, the trek to the lagoon seemed to drag on forever, an unending ordeal of gut-wrenching agony. His calf and thigh muscles were hurting when he finally stumbled from the shrub to the beach and lowered Chief Smith to the sand with a sigh of relief. He took ten seconds to catch his breath, then deposited the big man in the raft. "Now you can help," he said.

Alex stooped to the task of sliding the raft into the water, which was easily accomplished, and in short order Donovan had the outboard running and they were zipping across the deceptively serene lagoon toward the open sea and *Liberator.*

Immersed in reflection, mentally castigating himself for not taking a transceiver along, Donovan barely felt the salty spray moistening his skin. He'd neglected to take a transceiver along once before, when *Liberator* had put in at Dutch Harbor, and the landing party had nearly been cut off by white-shirts until Percy came to their rescue. Never again, he vowed, would he allow a shore party to leave the ship without a pocket transceiver, and he intended to issue an order to that effect.

The executive officer, who had been watching through binoculars, had four crewmen on hand to carry Chief Smith below. "What happened, Captain?" he asked as Donovan clambered from the raft. "Where's your brother?"

"Natives nabbed him. We're going after them right away."

"Right. I'll arm a shore party immediately," Percy said, and went to turn.

"Belay that," Donovan said.

"Sir?"

"They're in outriggers to the west of the atoll."

"Oh."

Donovan walked toward the hatch. "Have Flaze taken to sick bay. I want us under way in two minutes at flank speed."

"Aye, Captain."

Just beyond the rim of the horizon, far enough away so the *Charkov* couldn't be spotted visually by anyone on the American ship, the Soviet attack submarine floated on the surface, her seamen glued to their monitors, the SHADOW system fully engaged.

Standing in the control room, Captain Vazov clasped his hands behind his back and stared at the SHADOW's central core, watching the digital displays and the array of indicators. The computerized stalking system would automatically engage the helm the instant the *Liberator* moved from her current position. If the Vostoy veiling device continued to function flawlessly, the Americans would never know they were being pursued.

"I don't understand any of this, Comrade Captain," declared Serge Vatutin, standing to Vazov's right.

Which is par for the course, Vazov wanted to respond, but he wisely held his tongue, not even bothering to acknowledge the comment.

"Why are we playing games, Ivan? Why don't we finish the vermin off now?"

"I have already explained it to you."

"But it doesn't make sense."

Only because you are a fucking idiot, Vazov thought, and almost laughed.

"Aren't we taking too many risks? Shouldn't we destroy them before they detect our presence?" the political officer inquired nervously.

Vazov sighed and was about to respond when the SHADOW operator spoke up.

"The Americans are moving again, Captain."

"Bearing?"

"Due north. They are diving."

"Helmsman, monitor the SHADOW. Ensure we dive at the same rate and angle as they do."

"Yes, Captain."

"This is exactly what I mean," Vatutin said. "We should be sending the bastards to the bottom. Instead, we play children's games."

"All of our systems are functioning superbly. The Americans have no idea we are here. We are not taking any undue risks, Serge. We are performing a typical mission for which the *Charkov* was designed," Vazov explained patiently.

"I still say it is too dangerous."

"And *I* am still in command of this vessel."

"Target is levelling off at fifty meters," the helmsman declared. "They are circling the island."

"What are they up to now?" Vazov mused aloud.

"Who cares?" Vatutin muttered.

"I care, and so should you, my dear Comrade Captain," Vazov said. "Certainly, we could sink them now if we wished. But what would we have accomplished if we did?"

"Revenge."

"Which all of us want. But there is a method to this game, as you call it. Do you believe that the *Liberator* is the only American ship to have survived the war?"

"No, of course not."

"And if they aren't," Vazov went on, "does it not stand to reason that eventually they might rendezvous with other American warships?"

72

"I suppose so," the political officer conceded grudgingly.

"Then follow me on this," Vazov stated, more than a trace of anger creeping into his tone. "Since every man on board wants revenge, we should take the best revenge possible. Destroying the *Liberator* would be a great coup, but even greater would be destroying several American ships at once. Eventually the *Liberator* will unwittingly conduct us to other surviving vessels, and when she does, when we can send them all to the bottom of the ocean, we will make our move. We serve the Motherland better by eliminating as many enemy ships as possible, don't we?"

"Yes, Comrade Captain."

"So I trust you will refrain from any further criticism?"

"Of course," Vatutin said sullenly.

"Cheer up, Comrade," Vazov stated. "Our opportunity may come sooner than you expect. The *Liberator* would not have traveled all this distance without a reason. Why has she come to the Marshall Islands, if not to meet other ships? What can there possibly be here to interest her captain?"

"I don't know."

"Neither do I. And I am curious to find the reason."

Executive Officer Dragominov, who stood next to the sonar operator, glanced back at Vazov. "The *Liberator* has cleared the island and is bearing to the southwest."

"Good. Perhaps we will know their purpose soon."

"Their immediate goal seems to be apparent, Comrade Captain," Dragonimov said.

"What are they doing?"

"You won't believe me, Captain."

"Try me."

73

"The Americans are chasing four canoes."

Several seconds of silence ensured, and then the commanding officer cleared his throat.

"You're right. I don't believe it."

Cruising at 150 feet below the outriggers, *Liberator* paced the natives. Donovan had ordered their speed reduced to match that of the islanders, and the ship sailed along at a proverbial snail's pace.

"Why don't we surface right underneath them and give the buggers the scare of their life, sir?" Percy suggested, and grinned devilishly.

Not one to take the situation lightly when his brother's life hung in the balance, Donovan gave the executive officer a look of petty annoyance and said, "Because we'd dump Charlie into the drink along with the natives, and his hands are tied. One of them might even spear him. No, we'll continue as is for the time being."

Percy shrugged. "As you wish, Captain."

"Mr. Jennings, I want a fix on any land they could be heading for the moment you have one."

"Of course, Captain."

Donovan frowned and stared at the Cyclops, where the four outriggers were represented by diminutive icons, and fretted over Pirate's safety. Having Charlie on board had been a godsend, enabling him to cope just a little better with the unmitigated horror of the superpowers committing suicide and the appalling reality of the rest of his family and friends undoubtedly being dead, either burnt to a cinder in one of the firestorms or slain by the demented white-shirts. Only recently had he adjusted to the loss of his father. He couldn't stand the thought of losing Charlie, too.

The minutes dragged by, became a half hour.

Feeling like a bundle of nerves, Donovan shifted repeatedly in his chair. As he gazed glumly at the screen, he toyed with the idea of various options, everything from surfacing in front of the outriggers to dispatching a scuba squad, and discarded each idea as too hazardous for his brother's health. He welcomed the break in his comtemplation when Alex came onto the bridge and walked over to him. "How's Flaze?"

"He's conscious. Peter has him all patched up. The wound required only nine stitches."

"Only nine?"

"It looked a lot worse than it was," Alex said. "Peter doesn't believe that the chief has sustained a concussion, but he wants to keep Flaze in sick bay for twenty-four hours of observation."

"Fine by me."

"Flaze is giving Pete a hard time. He claims he's okay and doesn't want to stay in bed."

"When you go back, tell Flaze I said to stay in bed or else."

"Or else what?"

"He'll understand."

Alex faced the viewscreen. "Do we know where they're headed yet?"

"Not yet."

"How are you holding up?"

Donovan mustered a feeble grin. "As well as can be expected under the circumstances."

"Are you blaming yourself for Charlie's capture?"

"No. Why should I?"

"Just wondered," Alex said, leaning toward him, about to peck him on the cheek.

"Captain!" Communications Officer Jennings declared "We have land."

"How far?" Donovan asked, straightening.

"Ten miles dead ahead."

"Their home island, probably," Alex commented. "You're the expert on Micronesia. What will they do to Charlie when they get him there?" Donovan inquired.

"There are too many variables for me to make an accurate prediction. A lot depends on why they took him in the first place. Obviously, they're hostile, but to what degree? They must know about the war. Perhaps they blame us and they're taking their anger out on Charlie. Maybe they simply hate the white man. Most of the natives have adjusted to contact with the whites, but there are still a few holdovers from the blackbirder days, natives who haven't forgotten all the suffering we caused."

"Blackbirder?" Donovan repeated quizzically.

"Yeah. When explorers and traders first arrived in these islands, the natives referred to them as 'sailing gods.' Even though the natives had no resistance to all the diseases brought by the whites and the populations on many islands practically disappeared, friendly relations were maintained until the days of the slave traders, the 'blackbirders,'" Alex revealed. "The slavers wanted islanders to work on plantations in South America and Australia. Naturally, the natives refused to go, so the slavers took them anyway. There were a lot of hard feelings generated, and some of the islanders never forgot those terrible days."

"And they're still holding a grudge after all this time?"

"Let's put it this way: They're not very fond of us."

"Terrific."

"Chief Smith told me that three natives jumped Charlie and him without any warning. He was walking past a tree when one of them hit him with the branch, and he remembers sinking to his knees and seeing Charlie put up one hell of a fight, but the natives got hold of Pirate's weapon before he could fire. Then Flaze passed out."

Donovan rested his chin in his right hand, resolving on a course of action. "Mr. Hooper, flank speed to that island. Mr. Percy, organize a landing party of ten men, half armed with assault rifles and half with Franchis."

"Yes, sir!" Percy responded eagerly.

"With the possible exception of *Nemesis*, we're the dominant naval power in the South Pacific. It's damn time we started acting like it."

9

Ten times as large as the atoll, the natives' home island formed a boomerang shape with the curved ends pointing eastward. A gently sloping beach rimmed the eastern boundary, and several dozen outrigger canoes were arranged in rows above the water line along the middle stretch of sand. Beyond them rose a wall of vegetation, and beyond the forest rose an imposing and oddly sinister sight, the ravaged cone of an ancient volcano. The stark, jagged summit reared several hundred feet above the Pacific.

The ocean depth had drastically reduced the closer *Liberator* came to the island. Although the Pacific qualified as the largest and deepest ocean on the planet, with an average depth of 14,000 feet, the depth varied considerably due to the many ridges, plateaus, trenches, and guyots, flat-topped mountains that did not reach the surface. In the southwestern Pacific, where the ocean bed was cut by many high ridges and troughs, the fluctuation in depth varied even greater. One mile from the island the depth had been 8,000 feet. At a half mile, only 3,000. And at five hundred yards from shore the depth had decreased to 600 feet.

Fortunately the surface was calm, the wind light, typical of the conditions that had prompted the European discoverer of the ocean, Portuguese explorer Ferdinand Magellan, to name it Pacific, which meant "peaceful." Although the surface lay serenely, the same could not be said of Donovan's emotional state. Ordinarily the consummate professional, always reserved and in total control, Donovan could hardly sit still as the raft drew nearer to the beach.

Helmsman Hooper had brought the sub in close to the southern tip, and Donovan had ordered the three rafts to be launched. The crewmen applied themselves to the oars industriously, anxious to reach land before they could be spotted by the natives. Because he wanted Percy on the bridge in case *Nemesis* returned, Donovan led the rescue mission alone. He glanced over his right shoulder as the raft coasted onto the sand, in time to see *Liberator* submerging, and tapped the portable transceiver attached to his belt. Percy was under orders to keep the ship down until Donovan gave him the word.

"Let's hustle," Donovan directed, stepping onto the sand and hefting his Luigi Franchi.

The ten crewmen quickly pulled the rafts into the trees and huddled together, awaiting instructions.

"The canoe bearing my brother won't get here for at least thirty minutes," Donovan said. "We'll have plenty of time to get into position. Above all, we can't allow the natives on this island to spot us. There will be no firing unless I say so. Understood?"

A bobbing of heads attested to their comprehension.

"Fan out. Stay frosty," Donovan advised, and moved to the north, stepping lightly. The soft soil and the cushion of matted vegetation enabled his men to advance stealthily, and except for the occasional snap of a twig their passage was silent. The

Marines couldn't do any better, Donovan thought, and smiled.

Colorfully plumed birds frolicked in the trees, surprisingly vocal despite the proximity of the humans. Insects abounded, including beautiful, fluttering butterflies, some small, others astoundingly large. There were bright blue butterflies and scarlet butterflies, yellow ones and orange ones.

Donovan watched in fascination as a brown butterfly, its wings dotted with golden patterns, flew overhead. Its wingspread was easily ten inches. He'd had no idea that butterflies could grow so huge, and he wondered about the size of the indigenous spiders.

The lush tropical foliage, the proliferation of wildlife, the azure sky, and the picturesque beach all combined to imbue the scene with a Utopian quality. Shangri-la existed after all, right there in the South Pacific.

Donovan compared the paradisiacal setting to the devastation he'd beheld in Seattle and elsewhere, and he felt as if he had been transported to an alien world where symmetry and tranquility reigned. Such natural splendor, contrasted to the widespread destruction wrought by the hand of man, made him wonder if the human race deserved to be the masters of a world they had nearly destroyed.

In fifteen minutes they came within sight of the outrigger canoes at rest on the beach. A well-worn path led from the canoes toward the center of the island.

Puzzled by the absence of natives, Donovan paused ten feet from the path and crouched in the shelter of a coconut palm. Their village must be farther inland, he reasoned, which would work in his favor when it came time to snatch Charlie. Without reinforcements, the twelve natives who had taken Pirate should be easy to handle. He hoped.

The crewmen took cover only a few yards from the beach and settled down to wait.

After consulting his watch, Donovan gazed out to sea. He unclipped the transceiver and raised it to his lips. *"Liberator,* this is Donovan. How do you copy? Over."

Percy responded almost immediately. "Five by, Captain. Any problems?"

"Negative. We're in position and awaiting the outriggers."

"Jennings says you should be able to see them any second."

"Thanks. Any other targets? Any sign of *Nemesis?"*

"Negative on both counts."

"Excellent. If our twin should appear while we're ashore, you know what to do."

"Aye, Captain."

"Stay by the phone," Donovan quipped, and replaced the transceiver. With little better to do, he leaned against the tree and tried to relax. His roving eyes alighted on the distant figures of the outriggers. He thought of Charlie and reminisced on their childhood in New York City. As the oldest, many were the times he'd had to bail the ever adventurous Charlie out of trouble, and now here he was doing it once again. Old habits, evidently, really *were* hard to break.

Because of insufficient wind, the islanders had not bothered to unfurl the triangular sails topping the canoes. They were using oars, their brawny, powerful arms stroking in rhythmic precision, propelling the outriggers rapidly nearer.

Donovan waited until the canoes were fifty yards from shore before raising the transceiver again. *"Liberator?"*

"Percy here, Captain."

"Stand by. It won't be long."

"We're ready."

"I wish I had a camera to catch the look on their faces," Donovan said, and clicked off.

The four outriggers cleaved the water smoothly, knifing the final ten yards to the shore. With a lithe economy of movement, the natives vaulted out and brought their craft onto the beach. Two of the islanders hauled Charlie erect and deposited him upright on the sand. All of the natives retrieved their spears. The tall man prodded Charlie with his and gestured at the path.

"Quite poking me with that pigsticker," Charlie snapped.

Angered by the captive's effrontery, the tall native gave Charlie a shove, sending him shuffling in the right direction.

"Untie me and try that, bozo," Charlie said defiantly. He strode toward the path, his chin high.

Good old Pirate, ever true to form! Donovan thought, and whispered into the transceiver, "Now, Percy! Now!"

The natives were filing from the beach, with Charlie at their fore, when *Liberator* surfaced due east of the canoes, several hundred yards out, attended by a loud hissing caused by blowing her main ballast tanks. Several natives at the rear turned, saw the sub, and started yelling excitedly. All eyes focused on the teal hull glimmering in the sunlight.

Which was the moment Donovan had been waiting for. At a signal from him, two seamen darted from cover, grabbed a startled Charlie, and retreated into the forest again. The other crewmen covered them. Donovan smiled at his brother, then motioned with his right arm. Instantly, the landing party began to retrace its route to the south tip of the island.

Still engrossed in the spectacle at sea, enthralled by the huge sub and the men now moving about on the deck, the islanders gestured with their spears and jabbered.

Keep talking! Donovan's mind shrieked. Every second the natives were distracted meant another yard covered. He hoped to pull off the rescue without bloodshed, but he knew the islanders weren't about to permit the crew to leave unchallenged.

Charlie materialized next to Donovan's left elbow, his hands free thanks to one of the seamen, a Franchi clutched at waist level, a carefree smile on his face. "Thanks, Tom," he whispered.

"Just upholding the family tradition," Donovan responded.

They covered twenty yards before the inevitable transpired. The tall native looked over his shoulder and discovered Charlie was missing. Bellowing and waving his arms, he marshaled his companions and led them into the undergrowth. They glanced frantically all about, seeking their prisoner. A stocky, sharp-eyed fellow spotted one of the seamen and shouted.

The race was on.

"Go! Go!" Donovan ordered, all need for subterfuge gone. Wheeling, he joined his men in a general flight, slowing just long enough to speak distinctly into the transceiver. "Percy, they're on to us. Meet us at the pickup point!" He clipped the device to his belt and took off, Pirate still at his side.

Whooping loud enough to rouse the sleeping volcano, the natives bounded in pursuit. Their familiarity with the terrain, their years of experience as fleet-footed hunters, and their superb conditioning enabled them to close the gap swiftly, seemingly endowing their feet with wings.

83

Donovan was skirting a tree when a spear flashed from the rear and smacked into the trunk, its shaft quivering. He heard Charlie's Franchi chatter and kept going.

"We won't need to worry about him again," Pirate commented.

Gritting his teeth and breathing heavily, Donovan concentrated on pumping his legs. The escape devolved into a desperate foot race, and the outcome became readily apparent within the next few minutes.

"They're gaining," Charlie said.

Donovan risked a look, confirming the certainty of being overtaken, and glanced at his brother. "On me!"

Charlie simply nodded.

They sprinted another five yards, then Donovan stopped and pivoted, swinging the Franchi in an arc, squeezing the trigger and sending a hail of lead at the natives. He saw one drop, and the rest slowed.

Before the islanders could duck for cover, Charlie cut loose. In his hands, the hands of a master marksman, the Franchi burped in a lethal staccato and three of the natives were hurled to the turf, their torsos repeatedly perforated, two of them screaming as they convulsed and died.

"Move!" Donovan cried, and led the way southward again, counting on their tactic to delay the islanders for a while.

But it didn't.

Enraged by the loss of their companions, the remaining seven came on even faster, screeching at the top of their lungs, apparently resolved to catch the seamen at all costs.

For several minutes the landing party held their own, staying comfortably ahead of the natives. Then sustained flight began to take its toll. Sore thighs and tired leg muscles slowed reflexes, and although the crewmen were giving the race their all, a few of them started to flag.

Accustomed to the rugged existence endured by men and women who lived on the fringe of civilization, and imbued with the feral intensity of their primitive ancestors, the natives streaked across the ground with the fleetness of leaping deer.

Donovan scrutinized the landscape ahead, searching for a spot to make a temporary stand. The landing party outnumbered and outgunned the islanders. Routing the natives should be an easy task, and once they were put to flight the crewmen could retreat to the sub in safety.

A low knoll materialized sixty feet ahead, situated on the far side of an oval clearing.

Perfect. Donovan glanced to the right and the left, trying to draw the attention of his men. "The knoll!" he shouted. "On the knoll!"

Most of the seamen immediately understood. They angled toward the clearing, converging on their captain, a few firing random rounds at the islanders.

Donovan burst from the forest and kept going, waving for his men to close in, and they were halfway across the clearing when the first of the natives appeared and, without missing a step, launched his spear.

"Look out!" Charlie yelled.

The sun glinted off the metallic tip as the spear arced high, then slanted down, flashing toward the clustered seamen. They scattered, some diving and rolling, in a mad scramble to place themselves somewhere other than the spot the spear would hit. They succeeded, but a youthful crewman nearly lost a leg when the point thudded into the ground mere inches from his right thigh.

Charlie raised the Franchi and sighted on the

spear thrower, but the native wisely scurried behind a tree.

"To the knoll!" Donovan reiterated, leading the way and beckoning them onward.

More natives popped into view, and several charged after the sailors, oblivious to the fact they were now in the open and exposed.

Donovan attained the top of the knoll. He turned and aimed at the speediest of the natives. His shots weren't the only ones squeezed off. Several crewmen added the firing power of their weapons to his.

Three more islanders fell.

A surge of elation rippled through Donovan. With their numbers decimated, the four islanders still on their feet were fleeing. Suddenly, bewildering Donovan, he saw them halt and gaze to the west. Only then did he hear the chorus of upraised voices, the vociferous din of dozens of war whoops, and he swiveled in that direction. The short hairs at the nape of his neck prickled when he spied a large body of warriors streaming toward the knoll.

10

Reinforcements were the one element Donovan hadn't anticipated. He chided himself for his stupidity and motioned to the south. "Head for the rendezvous point!" he bellowed, and suited action to his words by racing from the knoll. Charlie and the seamen came after him, the sight of the onrushing horde lending strength to their tired limbs.

Seventy-five yards separated the two factions when the flight resumed.

How had the reinforcements arrived so quickly? Donovan speculated as he ran. Had a native hunting in the forest witnessed *Liberator* surface earlier and gone to rouse the village? Or had they simply heard the gunshots and responded en masse? In any event, the small landing party would be overwhelmed if he decided to try to make a stand. He needed a clever strategy, some way of holding the islanders at bay until the rafts could be launched back to the sub.

But what?

The crewmen conducted the foot race in grim silence, well aware of the consequences if they should be caught. None wasted rounds on the natives. They were saving every shot for the clinch.

An abrupt realization prompted Donovan to swerve to the left, to make for the beach. In the tropical forest his men had to contend with the added disadvantage of striving to down foes who could duck behind every available tree and shrub. But in the open, with their backs to the ocean, at least they would be able to see the islanders coming. "To the beach, men!" he cried.

The landing party slanted toward the Pacific Ocean, visible through the trees to the east. Also visible, her teal-colored hull the most welcome sight any of them had ever seen, was *Liberator*.

Two hundred yards from the island, Executive Officer Percy stared through a pair of high-resolution binoculars and scowled. He'd followed the progress of the battle as best he could, and he had ordered Helmsman Hooper to keep the ship abreast of the rescue party's position. Now he glanced at the helmsman and said, "Take her in as close as we dare."

"Aye, sir."

One of the junior officers gathered on the topside bridge cleared his throat. "We have to be careful how far in we go. We don't want to become stranded."

"Don't tell me my job, mister," Percy snapped, the binoculars over his eyes. He could see the landing party drawing nearer to the beach, and he grinned at the prospect of taking part in the fray. "I want ten seamen on the foredeck armed with assault rifles on the double!"

"Yes, sir."

Percy riveted his gaze on the twenty-foot-wide belt of beach and hoped he would be in time. Cover fire from *Liberator* might drive off the natives and enable Donovan to reach the rafts. He wished there was a .50-caliber machine gun mounted on the deck. Then he could *really* show those yapping bastards something!

"We may have a problem, sir," a junior officer noted.

"What kind?" Percy asked, looking over his right shoulder.

The man nodded to the north. "They're sending out a welcoming committee."

They? Percy swung around and was amazed to discover more natives manning the outriggers at the center of the eastern shoreline. "What do those fools think they're doing?" he muttered.

The answer became apparent moments later when eight of the canoes put to sea and bore in the direction of the sub. Behind them other outriggers were entering the surf.

"I think they plan to attack us," Hooper mentioned.

"Don't be ridiculous. They must know they can't harm us."

"Maybe not, sir," Hooper said.

"Haven't they heard of *Moby Dick?*" Percy declared sarcastically, and watched the canoes approach. *Liberator* was scarcely moving, creeping toward the beach. The islanders would easily overtake her.

Moments later the first of the ten seamen scrambled through the hatch and hastened to the foredeck. They took up their positions in a line from starboard to port, their assault rifles at the ready.

Percy glanced from the outriggers to the shore, where Captain Donovan and the landing party were engaged in a firefight, their backs to the water. He felt supremely confident the natives wouldn't be able to board the sub, if such was their intention, but he wouldn't be able to provide an effective cover fire for Donovan *and* repel the natives at the same time. The very idea that primitive South Pacific islanders could frustrate his design annoyed him no end.

This couldn't be happening!

89

"What are the Americans doing now?" Captain Vazov asked.

Executive Officer Dragominov looked at his superior. "From the transmissions we have intercepted, and I have verified the contents myself since I am fluent in English, they would appear to be attacking a native village."

"How very strange."

"If you ask me, all Americans are deranged," Serge Vatutin asserted. He stood, as ever, only a meter from Vazov. "They were always crazy. It must have been the political and economic indoctrination they were subjected to as children, all that emphasis on capitalism, on selfishness and greed. Such a blatant disregard for the higher ideals embodied in communism was bound to have a debilitating effect."

Vazov kept a straight face when he glanced at the political officer, knowing all too well that Vatutin sincerely meant every word. "They might be inclined to say the same about us."

"Sometimes, Comrade," Vatutin said stiffly, "being able to look at both sides of a picture can impair our reasoning."

Now what the hell was *that* supposed to mean? Vazov wondered, and simply nodded.

"Perhaps I could make a suggestion, Comrade Captain?" Vatutin asked.

"By all means, do."

"Why don't we attack now, while the Americans are preoccupied? With our SHADOW in operation, we can sneak right up on them and fire a torpedo right down their throats."

Vazov sighed. "We could, but we won't. Not until I am good and ready. Not until I am satisfied the Americans are not linking up with other warships.

Once I am satisfied of that, and one other thing, then we will finish off the *Liberator.*"

"What other thing, Comrade Captain?"

"Why in the world are they attacking a native village?"

Donovan was in deep shit.

The retreat to the rafts had been cut off by a large body of islanders who moved south along the edge of the forest and took up a position between the landing party and their sole means of returning to the sub, short of swimming. One hundred and fifty yards out, over a score of outrigger canoes were brazenly assaulting *Liberator,* the natives standing erect in their craft to hurl spears, war clubs, or long-handled axes. Although none of their weapons scored, and despite the loss of three canoes to automatic fire from the ten seamen, they persisted tenaciously and actually forced the crewmen to back off or be impaled.

On the beach the situation was no better. Dozens of islanders had the landing party pinned down at the water's edge. Spears occasionally streaked out at the sailors, but none came close to Donovan or his men. The natives stayed hidden in the vegetation, yelling at the top of their lungs and popping into view every now and then.

Their behavior mystified Donovan. What were they up to? he asked himself. They were deliberately holding back, as if they wanted to keep the landing party right where it was. Perhaps the natives were hoping the Franchis and assault rifles would run out of ammunition. If so, they were doomed to disappointment because Donovan cautioned his men against firing indiscriminately. "Only shoot when you have a target," he had instructed them.

After three minutes trapped on the beach, Charlie glanced at his brother. "Maybe we should rush the sons of bitches."

"We'd be slaughtered," Donovan responded. "At least now it's a standoff."

"But for how long?"

Donovan couldn't answer that question, so he gazed at the ship, at the uneven conflict still being waged. If anything, the natives were becoming bolder, driving their outriggers up against the sub's hull so they could toss their weapons with greater accuracy.

"What the hell is this action?" Charlie snapped.

Glancing at the jungle, Donovan was astounded to behold two natives emerging from cover with their arms in the air. Neither carried a weapon. "Don't fire!" he commanded instantly. "Hold your fire!"

"I don't trust them," Charlie said.

"You heard me," Donovan stated.

The pair advanced warily, clearly nervous but putting on a bold pretense. The islander on the right, the taller of the duo, had an arrogant swagger to his stride. He wore a beige cloth looped about his loins, a shell necklace, and an elaborate headdress. His stern countenance, more so than the headgear, indicated a man accustomed to authority, a person of prominence. His companion, shorter, stockier, and with a protruding abdomen the size of a watermelon, seemed to wish he could be somewhere else. His wide eyes roved over the seamen, always in motion, and he took smaller strides than his associate, dragging his feet. Grungy jeans clung to his stubby legs.

"I am Matal," the stern one stated in clipped English when he came within ten feet of the landing party, and halted.

"And I'm Captain Tom Donovan of the U.S.S.

Liberator. I demand that your people cease these hostilities at once."

A sly smile creased Matal's thin lips. "Hostilities?" he repeated, and gazed out at the outriggers swarming around the submarine. He clapped his hands twice, each time lowering his arms to shoulder height and sweeping them up again.

Donovan looked at the canoes. Shouts arose, a message passed from outrigger to outrigger, and in no time flat the natives had suspended their attack and were sitting quietly in their craft, their eyes on the beach.

"My people will not do anything unless I tell them to," Matal said, offering a fact, not boasting.

"If they do, you'll be burying warriors for a month," Donovan vowed, glaring at the native. "Are you their chief?"

"I am the head man in our village."

"And where'd you learn to speak English, bozo?" Charlie interjected.

"From one of the many missionaries who have visited my people. The missionaries have come for many, many years, trying to convert everyone to become Christian. They have set up churches and schools and taught us much."

"Evidently they forgot to teach you about hospitality," Charlie said.

"That's enough," Donovan stated.

Matal studied them for several seconds, finally focusing on Donovan. "The missionaries are all dead."

"What?"

"Their God was a false god. They told us their God was a god of peace and love, but now we know he is a god of war."

Donovan, aghast at the implication, took a step toward the leader. "You killed them?"

"We have returned to the old ways, the ways of

our ancestors. The sea is our Mother, and we worship her. She provides all that we need. And she does not say one thing and do another."

"But surely you didn't *kill* them?"

Matal's mouth curled downward. "The missionaries preached a religion of life, but now we know that your people live only to destroy. We saw the great fire in the sky far to the north of us, and we know that the radio broadcasts have all stopped."

"Did the missionaries give you a radio?" Donovan asked, realizing he wouldn't be able to extract any information concerning their fate.

"They gave us many things, and they have all turned out to be false."

"Why did your people attack my men?" Donovan demanded bluntly.

"Your people are no longer welcome in these waters."

"The Marshall Islands are a United States Trust Territory. We have a legal right to be here."

"Not anymore. My people no longer recognize your right. We rule ourselves."

"Do all of the natives in the Marshalls feel the same way?" Donovan inquired.

"I cannot speak for all the islanders," Matal said. "I can only speak for my people."

"Have you talked to any of the other islanders?"

"Yes."

"Where are they located?"

"That you must discover for yourself."

Donovan mulled the new information. Meager as it was, he now knew there definitely were other natives in the Marshalls and that some of them might be friendly. "We didn't come here to harm your people, Matal," he mentioned.

"Perhaps you speak the truth. But your people cannot be trusted and we want nothing to do with you."

"Then you shouldn't have attacked us."

"We will let you go in peace if you give us what we want."

Donovan and Charlie exchanged glances.

"I knew it," Pirate muttered.

"What do you want?" Donovan inquired.

"We would make a trade," Matal said.

"Go on."

"In return for letting you leave in peace, we ask for a token of your good will."

"What kind of token?" Donovan asked impatiently.

"Your guns."

Pirate's laughter brought a scowl to the native leader's face. "You've got to be kidding!"

"I am serious," Matal insisted. "We will let you leave if you will give us guns."

"I can't accept your terms," Donovan stated flatly.

"You'd just use the guns on us," Charlie said.

"No. I give you my word that we will not turn your own guns against you."

"Then why do you want them?" Donovan inquired. He gazed past the head man and saw at least three dozen warriors lined up at the edge of the tropical forest, apparently awaiting a signal from their leader.

"I will explain," Matal said. "We do not have any guns. My people have never had a need for them. But now we do. Now some of the clans to the south of us have told us we are no longer allowed to fish near their islands, and they chase us and kill us if we enter their territory. Some of those clans have guns. Not many, but having a few guns is better than having no guns at all."

Donovan pursed his lips, reflecting. Historically, many of the clans and tribes in Micronesia and Melanesia were hostile to one another. He recalled reading about a tribe of headhunters in the Solomons who were still surreptitiously taking the heads of their enemies right up to the turn of the century.

"We do not want much," Matal went on. "All we ask for are a few guns. With guns, my people can stop the other tribes from killing us. We can protect our village from their raids. Is this too much to ask?"

On the surface the request seemed reasonable, but Donovan wasn't about to grant it for two reasons. First, giving guns to this clan would upset the balance of power in that sector of the Marshalls. Matal's people must live in dread of an even more powerful tribe, which explained why Matal was so eager to deal with naval men who had slain a number of his followers. Second, despite the apparent elimination of the Department of Defense, the Pentagon, and the entire chain of command for the U.S. Navy, Donovan was a stickler for going by the book. And nowhere in the regulations did it state that trading arms to natives was under the province of a sub commander.

Matal had been staring intently at Donovan, reading the officer's expression. Now his dark eyes narrowed and he glared. "I take it that you will not give us the guns we need?"

Donovan saw no reason to beat around the bush. "No," he answered bluntly.

"We do not need your cooperation."

"Oh?"

"We can take the guns by force. We will kill every man with you and take all of your guns."

"And if you do, your village will be destroyed," Donovan informed him.

"Our whole village?"

"Every last man, woman, and child."

"And who would do such a thing? You will be dead."

97

Donovan pointed at *Liberator.* "That's a nuclear-powered submarine, Matal, armed with nuclear warheads. Surely you have heard about such ships?"

The islander stared at the teal hull.

"She can fire missiles that can burn your village to a cinder and fry all of your people to a crisp. Not one of you will be left alive. If you try to hide in the forest, she will destroy every tree and bush. That great fire you saw in the sky came from missiles exactly like hers."

Matal's forehead furrowed as he pondered the news.

"The man who is in charge of her right now is not the sort of man you want to make angry. He would like nothing more than to take revenge for our deaths, and if you slay us he will reduce your island to a wasteland," Donovan said earnestly.

"He would really kill the women and the children?"

"He'll show no mercy."

"Who is this mighty warrior?"

Donovan noticed his brother suddenly develop an interest in the sand, and he hoped Pirate wouldn't laugh and spoil everything. "He's our executive officer, John Percy."

"I would like to meet him."

"Perhaps that can be arranged at a later date. Right now, we want to return to our ship without interference from your people."

Matal took forever to make up his mind. He glanced from Donovan to the sub and back again while chewing on his lower lip. "You can go. But we would be honored if you would join us for a feast tonight at our village. The Nuranu people would be honored to show you their hospitality," he said, and looked meaningfully at Charlie.

"I'll let you know," Donovan responded.

"Please. We will not attack you again. You have my word on that."

"I'll let you know."

Matal, clearly displeased, made a gesture of resignation. "Very well. I will leave two of my men here. They both speak fair English. You can relay your answer through them."

"Fine," Donovan said.

With an imperious wave of his right hand, Matal wheeled and walked to the trees. He glanced back only once, at the outriggers floating near *Liberator,* and made a circle in the air. The next moment the trees swallowed him.

Donovan looked toward the ship and saw the canoes pulling away, then swept his men with a penetrating stare. "Let's get the hell out of here before they change their minds."

The policy session took place on the topside bridge. Donovan, his brother, Alex, Executive Officer Percy, Communications Officer Jennings, and Helmsman Hooper were all present. Hooper had maneuvered the sub to a point three hundred yards from shore, where they could keep an eye on the outriggers.

Pirate informally began the deliberations with an offhand comment. "I still can't believe those bastards let us go just like that."

"It wasn't just like that," Donovan said, snapping his fingers. "Matal let us go because he was afraid we'd blow his island to pieces. The only thing he understands is force."

"I wouldn't be so sure of that," Alex remarked.

"Okay. You're our science officer and our resident history expert. You know more about these people than any of us. You tell me why they let us go," Donovan responded.

"They may want to become our friends."

"Yeah. Right."

"Bear with me on this. Put yourself in their shoes—" Alex began.

"They don't wear any," Charlie interrupted.

"These are a proud, independent people we're dealing with," Alex resumed. "Yet they're not as belligerent and aggressive as some of the tribes in the Gilbert and Solomon islands. If they were, they would have kept coming at you until every last man had been killed. They have a code of conduct that might seem strange by our standards, but it's one they rigorously live by. If Matal invited you to a feast, then I'd say his offer is legitimate."

"And we just overlook the attacks?" Donovan countered.

"Not at all. But keep this in mind. Matal couldn't possibly have known about Charlie's abduction when he heard the gunfire and charged out of the village with all of his warriors. The ones who took Charlie were still on the beach. Did they have time to signal the village?"

"No. Not that I'm aware."

"So there you have it. As far as Matal was concerned, you were invading his island. Yet you said he didn't make an all-out effort to wipe out the landing party and he probably could have done so. Instead, once he had a fair idea of who you were, he declared a truce and made his offer. When you refused, did he continue the hostilities? No. He backed down and even invited us to a feast. I repeat. I think his offer is legitimate. At the very worst, he's hoping he can persuade you to part with the guns on a friendly basis rather than attempt to take them forcefully."

Donovan gazed at the dormant volcano. "To hear you tell it, the man is practically a saint."

"Is there something wrong with my scenario, some element I've missed?"

"No. You've succinctly covered all the bases. The way you've explained it, his actions almost seem justified."

"Not in my eyes," Percy spoke up. "Those natives attacked a U.S. Navy vessel, which is the same as attacking the United States. Their justification is irrelevant. I don't trust them."

"I'm with you," Charlie said. "You should have heard the things that crazy chief was saying."

"Like what?" Percy inquired.

"Like that business about you being a mighty warrior."

"What?"

"Didn't Tom tell you? Matal believes you're some kind of superwarrior. Tough as nails. He even wants to meet you."

Percy looked at Donovan. "Is this true, Captain?"

"Matal did make a few statements to that effect, yes."

"Why didn't you let me know, sir?"

Donovan shrugged. "It didn't seem important under the circumstances."

"Captain," Dave Jennings interjected.

"What is it?"

"Can you have Sensors checked again? I'm still reading that false contact every now and then."

"How often?"

"Twice today. Each time all I got was a fuzzy echo for a second. Damnedest thing I've ever seen."

"I'll have it taken care of," Donovan promised, then cocked his head. "Has there been any trace of *Nemesis* today?"

"None whatsoever, sir."

"Good. Hopefully they're off making someone else's life miserable for a change."

Peter Fisher's head popped out of the hatch and he smiled. "Sorry I'm late. But I was in the middle of a critical testing procedure and I couldn't cut it short." He climbed out and joined them.

"The radiation insanity?" Donovan asked.

"What else?" Peter rejoined.

"Are you still working on those tissue samples you took from the white-shirts who died in San Francisco?" Alex queried.

"Nope," Peter replied. "I've been working on tissue samples I took from Lisa."

To everyone's surprise, not the least being Helmsman Hooper's, Hooper suddenly blurted, "Lisa?"

Peter nodded. "I've discovered some interesting factors."

"Like what?" Donovan asked.

"I'll let you know when the data is more concrete, if it's all right with you. Right now I'm simply tracking down an intriguing discrepancy."

"Just let me know when you've found whatever you're looking for."

"Will do."

"Can you tear yourself away from your work long enough to attend a feast?" Alex inquired.

"A what?"

"The natives have invited us to a feast. But the prevailing consensus seems to be that we're nuts if we go."

Peter looked at the captain. "Do I have a vote in whether we go or not?"

"This isn't a democracy, but I did call all of you together to get your input," Donovan said. "Which reminds me. I rely on the chief a lot. How's he doing?"

"Griping up a storm. He can't wait to be cleared to return to duty. Lying in bed is driving him up the wall."

"I'll bet," Donovan commented. "Now what did you want to say about the feast?"

"I vote we go."

"Any compelling reason other than you're hungry for fresh fish?"

Peter nodded and faced the island. "I'd like to run as many tests as I can to determine the extent to which the inhabitants and the ecological chain have been tainted by the radiation. I can conduct blood, organ, and tissue sample tests on the natives. We have the capability to test the air, the water, and the plant life, so why not use it? Our computer projected that the South Pacific had been spared from the worst of the firestorms and the fallout. Here's our chance to ascertain exactly how much damage was done." He paused. "Oh, I know everything appears to be normal, but we all know that radiation often exhibits a long-term, cumulative effect. I vote we determine to what extent the local environment has been poisoned now, before we go to all the trouble of locating and building a base of operations."

Donovan shook his head and sighed.

"You don't agree?"

"Oh, I agree all right. It's just that between your sister and you, it's like debating Mr. Spock. Your logic doesn't leave any room for argument."

"So we're going, sir?" Percy asked hopefully.

"Not you, Mr. Percy. I'll need you on the bridge."

"But, sir—"

"There are no buts about it," Donovan cut him off. "Mr. Percy, I've succeeded in convincing their chief that you are the meanest son of a bitch in this ocean or any ocean. Matal believes you'll nuke them if they look at us crossways. You're my ace in the hole. So long as they know that you're out here ready to press the button, they're not likely to cause us any trouble. I'm sorry. I know you'd like to go. But you'll have to remain on board as a security precaution."

103

"Aye, Captain."

Charlie snickered. "This is just great. We're going to a native feast where we might wind up as the main course."

Alex laughed and gave his shoulder a playful shove. "I doubt that. There's no conclusive evidence that these islanders ever practiced cannibalism."

"That's a relief."

"Some of them did engage in human sacrifice, though."

"They did?"

"Yes. But that was ages ago. And they were very selective about the practice. They only offered their sacrifices at certain times," Alex said, and winked at Donovan.

"Like when?" Charlie wanted to know.

"Oh, usually at their feasts."

Charlie sneered at the sporty green. We're ing to a native feast. We shouldn't wind up the main course.

Alex laughed and to put another a playv

12

There were a dozen natives waiting to escort the party from *Liberator* to the feast. Each wore his finest regalia for the occasion. Gone were the tattered jeans and other vestiges of Western civilization. Their apparel consisted of elaborately painted tunics constructed from tightly interwoven plant fibers, and simple loincloths. Each man wore an ornamental wooden comb in his hair, and each had applied white streaks to his forehead, cheeks, and legs. Perhaps as a concession to the Americans, none of the escorts were armed.

The shore party consisted of Donovan, Pirate, Alex and her brother, Communications Officer Dave Jennings, who wore a transceiver clipped to his belt, and two junior officers. Many others wanted to come, but Donovan had reluctantly refused them permission on the grounds that the Nuranus might have a trick up their collective sleeve, and the fewer crew members who were exposed to danger, the better.

"I wish we'd brought along a Franchi or an assault rifle," Charlie mentioned as he stepped from the raft.

"Why put temptation in their reach?" Donovan responded. "We'll have to make do with sidearms." As an added precaution, he had decided to issue only pistols to the shore party, fully cognizant of the risk he ran should Matal's invitation turn out to be a trap.

A beefy islander approached and bowed his head. "I am Pelua. Matal says bring you to our village."

"Thank you. We're looking forward to the feast," Donovan said. He debated on whether to turn around, return to the ship, and forget the whole thing. If any harm came to the members of the shore party, he would have to bear the ultimate responsibility. But he couldn't afford to pass up the opportunity to establish friendly relations with the islanders. If *Liberator*'s base of operations was to be located in the Marshalls, he wanted as few enemies lurking on his doorstep as possible.

"Come with us, please," Pelua said, and gestured at the path near the outrigger canoes.

Donovan surveyed the virginal island, admiring the golden glow cast on the lush vegetation by the setting sun. The sunlight outlined the cone of the volcano in stark relief, lending the setting a primordial aspect. He fancied that at any second a dinosaur might lumber out of the tropical jungle. "Let's go," he announced, and followed Pelua, who quickly moved about eight feet ahead.

Alex came up on his right. "I want you to behave yourself at the village."

"How do you mean?"

She grinned and touched his hand. "You'll understand when we get there."

Donovan looked over his right shoulder and caught the eye of Dave Jennings, then nodded, a mere bob of his chin.

The communications officer reached down and pressed the transmit button on his transceiver. Percy would be monitoring the open channel the entire time they were on the island.

Pleased by his devious subterfuge, Donovan hiked

106

deeper into the trees. He still had his transceiver with him, adjusted to a different frequency so Percy could raise him in an emergency. Until he trusted the Nuranus, he had no intention of letting his guard down.

"Isn't this marvelous?" Alex asked, gazing at the pink-and-saffron-infused horizon.

"It is beautiful," Donovan admitted.

"No wonder so many painters and writers thought so highly of the South Pacific. Even the sunsets are awe-inspiring."

"Have you ever done any painting or writing yourself?"

"I've dabbled," Alex said. "Which is why I've concentrated my line of work on computers. I'm not all that artistic, although I would have loved to have been living back in the days of Paul Gauguin, when he painted his famous canvases in Polynesia."

"Wasn't there a play based on these islands?"

"Rogers and Hammerstein's *South Pacific.* But it's a little-known fact that their play was actually based on the novel *Tales of the South Pacific* by James Michener."

"Wasn't he the guy who wrote those thick, thick books?"

Alex glanced at him. "You're putting me on, right?"

"A little."

"Michener wasn't the only writer to base his work on the South Seas. Herman Melville, the guy who wrote *Moby Dick,* wrote two books about this region. Neither were ever as popular, though."

"Probably because he didn't include the whale."

"You certainly are displaying a callous disregard for higher literature," Alex quipped.

"You think so?" Donovan responded. "Well, it just so happens that there is one book about the

South Pacific that I happen to have read three times."

"Really?" Alex said, and pondered for half a minute before the obvious occurred to her. *"Mutiny on the Bounty.* It figures you'd like a book dealing with a ship and the sea."

"The book deals with a great many issues. To a Navy man, the subject of mutiny is intensely fascinating. Mutiny is one of the gravest military offenses, punishable by death. At one time or another we all ask ourselves what we would do if we were caught up in a mutinous situation. If I ever find the time, maybe I'll read it again."

Alex gazed at their guide as they wound among the trees, bearing to the west, directly toward the volcano. She inhaled the dank air and felt a slight breeze on her face. The beautiful surroundings were almost enough to make her forget about the horror of the war and its aftermath. Almost, but not quite. She heard footsteps behind her, and then her brother caught up with them.

"Do you think we could stop so I can take some samples?" Peter inquired. Slung over his right shoulder was a large brown leather bag containing the equipment he would need to conduct his tests.

"Not yet," Donovan advised him. "We don't want to keep our host waiting. Once we're at the village I'll ask his permission." He lowered his voice to ensure Pelua couldn't overhear. "Besides, it'll flatter Matal's ego if I go through the motions. We need to go out of our way to be on good terms with these people. They might be able to do us a service later."

The path began to climb a gradual grade. The soil underfoot was soft, almost spongy. The jungle on both sides became denser and filled with shadows. Paying their last tribute to the waning day, the birds were in full cry, their calls blending into a raucous natural concerto.

108

"This is magnificent," Peter commented. "Will our island be anything like this one?"

"I hope so," Alex said.

"The island we finally settle on will depend on the availability of a deep-water port for the ship," Donovan responded. "I'm more interested in our safety than our comfort."

"Spoilsport," came from Alex.

"Do you know of any specific islands that will fit the bill?" Peter inquired.

"No. Our library contains as much information on the Marshalls, and every other chain in the South Pacific for that matter, as any library in existence before the war. We've fed it all through the Cray-9 and came up empty-handed. Our only recourse is to go from island to island until we locate the ideal site."

"And how long will that take?"

"Months."

"I'm in no hurry," Alex interjected. "Do you realize how much money I'm saving?"

"Money?" Donovan repeated quizzically.

"Yeah. A tour of the entire South Pacific would have cost a small fortune just a few months ago."

Donovan and Peter both chuckled.

After several hundred yards the grade tapered off and became a narrow plain bordered on the south and west by luxuriant rain forest and on the north by the volcano. Situated in the center of the plain was the native village, dozens of houses arranged around a central open space. The buildings were a curious mixture, with about half of them having been built of thatch on stone platforms and the rest being rectangular wood-frame homes with fiber walls. All of the houses had thatch roofs except a large one near the middle, a wood-frame affair with a corrugated-iron roof.

Over a hundred natives were gathered to welcome the shore party, and the sexes were more or less equally represented. The children hung in the background, giggling and staring wide-eyed at the newcomers. All of the men wore their best garb. And the women, many of whom were stunningly lovely, wore knee-length skirts made from split coconut leaves or fiber, necklaces and bracelets of shell or coconut rings—and nothing else. From the waist up they were naked.

Charlie suddenly stopped and gawked. "I think I've died and gone to heaven."

"Put your tongue back in your mouth," Donovan chastised him. "Remember, you're to be on your best behavior." He did a double take and glanced at Alex. "So that's what you meant?"

"It's quite common for the men and the women in the South Pacific to go around naked on top, although they will dress up on special occasions. I knew what to expect and didn't want you to make a fool of yourself by drooling all over the ladies."

"Charlie's the one you have to worry about."

"Poor Charlie seems to be in a daze," Dave Jennings commented.

The islanders had formed into a crescent shape at the outskirts of their village. Standing at the front, wearing the most regal trappings of all, was Matal. His arms were folded across his chest, and a flowing fiber cape shrouded his broad shoulders and fell almost to the ground.

Pelua hurried toward the chief.

"Well, here goes nothing," Donovan muttered, and led his party forward slowly, acutely conscious of the staring islanders. He noticed that none of them were bearing arms, and he came to the conclusion that Matal must be bending over backwards to demonstrate the Nuranus' peaceful intentions.

The leader and Pelua exchanged a few words in

their own dialect. Matal looked at Donovan and smiled. "Welcome to our village. My people are quite pleased you decided to accept our invitation."

"So it would seem."

"We will eat and drink and talk long into the night. We have much to discuss."

"We do?"

"Assuredly," Matal said, and gestured with his left arm. The people immediately parted, opening an avenue through their midst. "Come. Walk with me."

Donovan did as protocol required and stepped to the chief's right. Together they moved toward the center of the village. Surrounded by a sea of smiling, alien faces, Donovan felt goose bumps on his flesh. If the Nuranus were going to be treacherous, now would be the time.

"When you spoke with a loud voice to my men on the beach earlier, it made my heart happy to learn that you had accepted our invitation."

"We wouldn't have missed this for the world."

"How did you do it?"

"What?"

"Speak with a loud voice. My men told me that your ship was far from shore and yet they could hear you clearly."

"I spoke through a microphone," Donovan disclosed. "Electronic circuits amplified my voice."

"You must show me how it is done sometime."

Donovan prudently said nothing.

"Is the one you call Percy with you?" Matal inquired, gazing over his left shoulder at the other members of the party.

"No. Executive Officer Percy remained on board our ship. He sent his regards."

"You told him about me?"

"We discussed you at length, yes," Donovan replied, and was surprised when the head man seemed pleased by the news.

"I hope I will get to meet him tomorrow."

"Tomorrow?"

Matal unexpectedly halted. "Yes. Are you planning to leave before then?"

"I hadn't really considered our departure time yet," Donovan said. "It all depends."

"I hope you will stay a few days, at least, so we may conclude our business."

"What business are you referring to?"

"I have been thinking over the things I said to you when we met, and I must apologize for my harsh words. I was wrong about you not being welcome in these waters. My people want to be your friends."

"You've had a remarkable change of heart. Earlier today your people were trying their damnedest to kill us, and now you say we should be friends," Donovan said, and paused. "I hope you won't be offended if I have a hard time believing you." A full ten seconds of uncomfortable silence followed his remark, and he wondered if he had insulted the head man and what the consequences might be. If the Nuranus turned hostile and attacked without warning, Percy was bound to hear the commotion on the open channel between Dave Jennings's transceiver and the ship. But by the time the executive officer could bring a rescue party, it might be all over.

Matal uttered a protracted sigh. "I was afraid you would feel this way."

"Have I insulted you?"

"No. If I were you, I would feel the same way." Matal added a string of harsh words in his dialect, then caught himself and looked at Donovan. "I am sorry. All this has happened because of Tamel, and I become angry when I think of him."

"Who?"

"Tamel was the one who attacked the two men from your ship on Eyoka, the island east of ours. He talked those with him into bringing one of your men back here. All this was unknown to me. I did not know you were in these waters until a lookout on the volcano saw your ship come to the surface. We did not know who you were or what you wanted, so the men gathered and moved toward the shore. We heard gunfire and rushed to defend our island, and we drove your men to the beach," Matal related. "We could have killed you, but by then I had the facts from Tamel. That is why we spared you."

"For which I'm grateful," Donovan said.

"Because of that fool Tamel, eight of our warriors were killed and nine are injured."

"I'm sorry," Donovan said mechanically, not knowing what else he could say under the circumstances.

"The fault was Tamel's, not yours. His actions made many of our women widows and greatly weakened our clan."

Donovan expected the head man to launch into another pitch for guns. Instead, Matal gazed thoughtfully at the open space in the middle of the village. "I've brought our doctor along," Donovan mentioned. "He'd be happy to take a look at your wounded."

"Yes, that would be nice. Thank you."

They covered another ten yards before Matal spoke again.

"Our ways are not your ways, Donovan. They never have been. Many of the islanders tried to live as the whites live, and all they saw for their efforts was poverty and shame. We were born to be one with the sea, and not all the government and mis-

113

sion schools in the world could make us other than what we are."

Impressed by the native's sincerity, Donovan listened attentively. There seemed to be a side to Matal's character he hadn't anticipated, a touch of the philosopher in the primitive.

"But it has ever been that way. In early times, when the whites first came to these islands, our ancestors greeted them with open arms. And what did they get in return? Diseases and slave ships. In recent times, when the whites built huge cities where the rich came to lay in the sun, many of our people went to those cities to find work and wound up living in slums."

Donovan stared straight ahead and spied native women busily scurrying about the open area, engaged in preparing the feast. The tasty aroma of food being cooked reached his nostrils.

"Why must your people destroy everything?"

The unexpected question drew Donovan up short. "We don't destroy *everything*," he responded, a bit more defensively than he intended.

"Your people have almost destroyed the world. What more is left?" Matal countered somberly. "You were right, Donovan. I have heard about such things as nuclear warheads. The teachers at the mission schools taught us all about the wonders of your civilization. How the Russians and the United States could wipe each other out with their missiles and bombs. I never became concerned because both countries are so far from the South Pacific. I never appreciated how crazy both sides truly were."

"The war might not have been the faults of the U.S. We don't know who started the fireworks."

Matal glanced at the captain. "Is that an excuse?"

Donovan shook his head. The chief had turned out to not be so primitive after all. Or so he thought

114

until several minutes later, after the entire population of the village had gathered in the central area and the shore party had taken their seats on fiber mats situated near the west end. A chair made from woven reeds had been positioned at the head of the mats, and the chief sat down and surveyed those he led. He addressed them for five minutes, speaking authoritatively, eliciting nods occasionally, and once every man, woman, and child stomped their right foot several times in a row.

Alex, who was seated on Donovan's right, leaned toward him and whispered, "I wish I spoke their dialect."

Across from Donovan sat Charlie, and he couldn't seem to take his eyes off the native women. When one of them knelt near him to deposit a tray containing coconut, breadfruit, and yams, and her pendulous breasts swayed back and forth within arm's reach, his eyes threatened to bulge out of their sockets.

When Matal finished his speech, he stared at Donovan. "I told them that tonight they have a chance to make amends for the trouble we caused you. I told them that you have come here in peace, and that our two peoples can live in friendship. Tonight, our village is your village. Anything you want is yours."

"Anything?" Charlie responded, glancing at one of the women.

A smile creased the head man's lips. "Anything. If, of course, she is not married. In the early times my people were not as concerned about such things. But the missionaries taught us that a man and wife should always be faithful, and for decades we have tried to live as they wanted." He paused. "I have often wondered why we listened to them when they made our lives so miserable. They took all the fun out of our lives and put rules there instead. Rules are meant for those who don't want to enjoy life."

"I never thought of it quite that way before," Donovan said. As a career Navy man, he viewed rules as essential to proper conduct and the maintenance of discipline. If all rules were thrown out the window, military decorum would fall to pieces.

The native women continued to bring trays of food. Cooked fish and steaming crabs were in abundance. So were bananas and plantains. Earthen vessels were filled to the brim with various brews. Exotic dishes, the likes of which none of the shore party had ever seen before, were spread in a row along the ground.

"You may begin eating whenever you like," Matal informed Donovan. "There is no waiting on ceremony."

"Your people have certainly gone to a lot of effort to make this meal."

"They are used to it. We feast at least once a month. This one is special because you are our guests. Eat your fill. Later there will be entertainment."

"Dancing?" Charlie asked.

Matal smiled and nodded.

"I can hardly wait," Charlie said.

"Before we go too far, I would like to give you a gift," the chief stated.

"You don't have to," Donovan responded.

"Yes, I do. This gift is a token of our sincerity. To show that I mean what I say when I tell you that we would like to be your friends, I had this set aside," Matal said. He clapped his hands and a young woman appeared bearing a covered tray. She walked up to Donovan, bowed, and placed the tray at his feet.

"You may open it," Matal said.

Thinking he was about to unveil a tantalizing

dish, or perhaps a valuable object, Donovan took hold of the tray cover and lifted. His eyes widened and he inadvertently gasped in astonishment. For there, propped on the tray, was a severed human head.

13

"Dear God!" Alex blurted.

"Son of a bitch!" came from Pirate.

Donovan stared at the head in fascination, noting the strands of flesh dangling under the chin, the protruding, discolored tongue, and the crimson splotches dotting the victim's chin and cheeks. The man's features looked oddly familiar. "I trust this isn't your idea of a joke."

"No, it is my idea of how to prove to you that we do not want to harm you."

"I don't understand."

"Say hello to Tamel."

And suddenly Donovan knew where he had seen the man before. The head belonged to the tall native he'd observed on Eyoka, the one in the black pants who had appeared to be in charge. So this was the price a man paid for transgressing the will of the chief in an aboriginal society! He gazed at Matal with newfound insight into the other's psyche.

"Have I upset you?"

"This wasn't necessary."

"For us it was. How else could we convince you that not all the Nuranus think as Tamel did? He has been punished, and his punishment was just.

118

Thanks to him, we lost many good men. His head was empty in life, so he will not miss it in death."

Donovan's lips compressed. In a crude sort of way, Matal made sense. Tamel's actions were akin to a mutiny on board a ship. A situation any captain was empowered to handle as he saw fit, even to the extreme measure of putting the mutineers to death. If he judged Matal to be in the wrong, then he was applying a double standard. How could he morally justify the taking of lives by so-called civilized men, yet condemn a similar action by those who did not subscribe to the same set of rules? Especially now that the "civilized men" had blown the rules and nearly everything else to smithereens?

"If I have offended you, I am sorry," Matal said.

"You haven't," Donovan assured him. "But I'd be grateful if you could have the head removed."

"Of course." Matal clapped again, and the same young woman hurried over to his chair. He gave her instructions, and she promptly took the tray away. "Is that better?"

"Much, thank you."

"Tamel's body is feeding the fishes. I can have it shown to you, if you wish."

"That won't be necessary," Donovan assured him. He gazed at the food, and suddenly his hunger had evaporated.

"Do you believe me now?" Matal asked.

"I believe you."

"Can our two peoples be friends?"

"Only time will tell," Donovan answered.

"If we may help you in any way, you have only to ask. As you can see, we grow more food than we use. You would be welcome to share with us."

"Thanks for the offer," Donovan said, surprised yet again that Matal made no mention of the guns. He still suspected there must be an ulterior motive to the abrupt about-face the Nuranus had done.

The feast slowly got under way, with the island-ers exhibiting an uncharacteristic reserved atti-tude and the shore party emotionally restrained because of the beheading and their latent suspi-cions. After a half hour, after the natives had im-bibed sufficient quantities of their favorite drink, a potent beverage called *siva* that tasted pleasantly sweet to the guests and packed the intoxicating punch of the best moonshine, everyone began to re-lax and the festivities launched into full swing.

Donovan ate just enough food to be polite. He no-ticed that Charlie and Alex dug into their meals with gusto, and Pirate in particular seemed to be trying to stuff himself until he burst. At one point Donovan noticed Peter Fisher looking at him, and the moment he did Peter tapped the brown leather bag lying next to his right leg. Understanding, Donovan nodded and glanced at the head man.

"Matal, with your permission we would like to conduct a series of tests to determine to what ex-tent your people and your island have been affected by the war."

"What kind of tests?"

"Oh, soil, water, and blood tests. Things like that. We believe the South Pacific to be relatively radi-ation free, and the readings by our instruments on the ship confirm our belief. These new tests would enable us to measure certain effects precisely."

"You may take your tests whenever you like."

"Thank you. And when may our doctor look at your wounded?"

"As soon as our feast is over," Matal said, and motioned at a man standing nearby. He said a few words in his own tongue, then translated for the benefit of the Americans. "The dancing will begin."

"All right!" Charlie declared.

In short order a wide space was cleared. Torches were lit to compensate for the dwindling twilight.

Twenty islanders, all robust warriors, stepped into the space and formed into four rows, facing the shore party.

Charlie did a double take and glanced at the chief. "The men do the dancing?"

"Of course. Some clans allow their women to dance, but we stick to the old ways."

"Lucky us."

Donovan almost laughed at the comical expression on his brother. He took a sip of *siva,* then lit a Lucky Strike and inhaled deeply. He could finally feel himself beginning to relax, to enjoy the evening, and he focused on the dancers as the assembled islanders gave voice to a lively chant and a half dozen men commenced beating on handcrafted drums. The dancers broke into a slow, graceful shuffle, moving in unison, and swept their arms from side to side, then started stamping their feet in rhythm to the drum beat. In the flickering glow from the torches, their shadows undulated across the assembled watchers.

A feeling of lassitude crept over Donovan, and the more he sipped at the *siva* the more the feeling grew. For the first time since before the war, he felt almost at peace with the world, strangely at ease despite being surrounded by potentially dangerous natives. He watched the dance and tapped his right hand on his knee in time to the pounding of the drums. The twenty men were performing high, vaulting leaps, spinning in midair to reverse their positions, and alighting on the balls of their feet with all the suppleness of jungle cats.

Matal unexpectedly materialized on Donovan's left and sat down. He leaned close so he could be heard. "May I ask you a question, Captain?"

"Certainly," Donovan replied, forcing himself to concentrate, to ignore the pleasant sensation the

121

siva induced. He wondered if the guns would be the topic of conversation.

"Have you ever been afraid?"

The question made Donovan blink a few times in perplexity. "A few times," he admitted. "Why?"

"Because I am very afraid. I'm afraid for our clan, for our future. Do you want to know the real reason I invited you here tonight, the real reason I didn't have your party wiped out today?"

"Sure."

"Because you may have the answers I need, Donovan. I know more about the outside world than most of my clan. I know a little about nuclear warheads, as I told you," Matal said, and paused. "What have your people done to the world? How bad is it? What will happen to my people? Not tomorrow or the next day, but a year from now. Are we really radiation free, as you put it?"

"We believe—" Donovan began, then fell silent when a most amazing event transpired.

The ground began to bounce up and down, almost as if the earth itself had elected to participate in the dance. The islanders suddenly froze. All of the homes swayed slightly. And from off to the north came a series of booming retorts, drowning out the beating of the drums.

Matal's eyes widened and he leaped to his feet.

Stunned, Donovan dropped his drink and tried to emulate the chief. The violent jiggling caused him to slip as he went to push erect, and he would have fallen if not for Matal, who grabbed his right arm and supported him. "Thanks."

"We are doomed."

"An earthquake isn't the end of the world."

"This is not an earthquake," Matal said, and pointed past Donovan's right shoulder.

Still feeling the effect of the native brew, his senses sluggish to respond to the situation, Donovan pivoted and gaped in consternation at the volcano. The suddenly active volcano. A reddish halo hung over the towering cone, and columns of smoke gushed high into the sky. "Has this ever happened before?" he queried anxiously.

"Never."

"Damn."

"Take your people to your ship," Matal stated.

"And what about you?"

"My people will take to our boats and put out to sea."

"Do you have enough canoes for everyone?" Donovan asked.

Matal glanced at his spellbound tribe. "We will take care of ourselves. Go, Captain. Go before it is too late."

"We can help you evacuate."

"Go," Matal insisted, and placed his hand on Donovan's shoulder. "Thank you, though. And I am sorry."

"For what?"

Without bothering to respond, the head man moved off, shouting commands, galvanizing his clan into action.

Alex, Pirate, Peter, Dave Jennings, and the pair of junior officers clustered around Donovan.

"What's the word?" Charlie asked.

"Back to the sub. Pronto."

"What about the natives? We can lend a hand," Alex suggested.

"They don't want our help. Let's go."

Donovan led the way, threading a route through the islanders, many of whom were still gawking at the crimson haze illuminating the northern sky. The quaking had subsided, although ominous rumblings emanated from the volcano.

"Maybe it won't blow," Alex said.

"Better safe than sorry," Donovan said, and

whipped his transceiver from his belt. *"Liberator,* this is Donovan. Do you read me?"

"Loud and clear, Captain," Executive Officer Percy acknowledged. "I'm on the topside bridge and I'm watching the volcano. We're pulling in as near as we can to the shore."

"Good man. We're on our way back. As soon as we're aboard, we'll head for deeper water."

"Aye, Captain. Our readings indicate a geothermal increase. Nine hundred and seventy degrees already."

"Any underwater activity?"

"Negative, Captain."

"Keep your eyes peeled," Donovan said, and broke into a run when he passed the last of the villagers. A bright light flared behind him and he looked back, dreading the worst, to find his brother holding a flickering torch.

"This might come in handy," Charlie said.

They found the path and hastened eastward. On both sides the jungle presented twin walls of inky shadows. Silent as a tomb, not even the birds squawked. The breeze rustled the foliage, providing a backdrop of constant low swishing, as if a legion of ghosts whispered among the trees.

"I won't get to take my samples," Peter lamented.

"There will always be another day," Alex told him.

"Maybe not for this island."

Donovan slowed on the grade, not wanting to lose his footing and pitch into the vegetation. He wondered if there would be other active volcanoes in the Marshall Islands and elsewhere in the South Pacific. The Cray-9 had projected that such would be the case. The best scenario indicated volcanism had increased dramatically, but not to the extent of imperiling all life in the region. Donovan hoped the computer was right.

Since most volcanoes were located in areas where the earth's crust had been weakened, volcanic systems tended to exist in belts of greatest activity. The Circum-Pacific system, of which the Marshalls were a part, also included the volcanoes of Japan, the Philippines, the Indonesian islands, and New Zealand. Everywhere *Liberator* went in the South Pacific, the threat of a volcanic eruption loomed as an ever present possibility.

Life on the precipice, Donovan thought, and negotiated a curve in the trail. He spotted *Liberator,* her running lights on as Percy brought her in, and grinned in relief. As if echoing his sentiments, Charlie made a comment.

"Man, does that sub look good!"

Prompted onward by the rumblings from the cone, the shore party sped to the beach and launched the two rafts that had carried them to shore. Crewmen were waiting on the sub to assist them in climbing onto the deck. Donovan jogged to the topside bridge, where he found Percy staring at the island through binoculars.

"Captain."

"Anything new?"

"The temperature in that baby has risen to eleven hundred degrees."

"Get us the hell out of here."

Percy barked an order into the intercom and the helmsman on duty headed for the open ocean at flank speed.

The reddish glow above the volcano's main vent had brightened, bathing the island in its radiance and illuminating the spiraling smoke formations. A few bright specks, flaming cinders or volcanic bombs known as lapilli, arced from the crater.

"You were lucky you got out of there when you did, sir," Percy mentioned.

"Let's hope the islanders are equally as lucky," Donovan said. He took the binoculars and adjusted the lens to his eyes. Scores of orange pinpoints appeared back in the jungle and grew rapidly larger. He identified them as torches and hope welled within him. Another ten minutes and Matal would have his people out to sea. "Come on," he said to himself. "Move it!"

"Captain?"

"Nothing."

More and more volcanic bombs were flying in all directions, resembling streaking meteorites as they plummeted to the ground. Most landed on the island, although several splashed into the water close to shore.

"Should we submerge, sir?" Percy inquired.

"Not yet."

"Should I sound alert stations?"

"Not yet."

"Begging the Captain's pardon, but don't we run a risk if we stay on the surface?"

Donovan nodded at the island. "As long as there is a chance that we can help those people, we'll continue as is."

"But what can we do for them, sir?"

"I won't know that until the opportunity arises. And I would strongly suggest that you drop the subject."

"Aye, Captain. May I say that I certainly hope you know what you're doing?"

"You may."

A sound much like an explosion drew their attention to the volcano.

"She's getting set to blow," Percy commented, more on a hunch than any scientific knowledge about volcanoes.

126

Donovan pressed the binoculars to his eyes again. The natives had narrowed the distance to the beach, but they still had so far to go. He could make out the leading figures as they hastened down the last leg, a straight stretch a hundred yards long, and he thought he could distinguish the tall figure of Matal, who seemed to be carrying a child. "Hurry," he whispered. "Damn it all, hurry!"

The islanders tried. But they were fifty yards from their outrigger canoes when a thunderous roar rent the air.

14

The eruption was spectacular.

The top of the volcano blew to pieces as tremendous blasts of steam shot out of the crater and rose several thousand feet into the sky. Red flames rose heavenward and arched around the rim. Mixed with the steam and fire were combustible gases, rocks, and ashes, strewn every which way.

Donovan stood riveted to the topside deck, scarcely breathing, watching the tableau unfold. He saw Matal leading the natives in a mad dash for the canoes, and for several seconds he believed they would make it.

Another mighty discharge shook the entire island, and the side of the volcano was ripped out. A blanket of scorching flame hurled from the depths and plunged downward, enveloping the cone and sweeping down upon the village, instantly incinerating every home; the wood-frame homes and the thatch houses alike burnt to a crisp in the space of a heartbeat.

"Dear God!" Donovan breathed.

The wall of fire continued to spread outward from the cone, consuming the verdant jungle, every last twig, as if it consisted of dry tinder instead of lush plant life. Roaring constantly, the solid shroud of flame rolled in a mass right down to the shore, overtaking the fleeing islanders and engulfing them before any of them could utter so much as a terrified shriek.

Only when the irresistible volcanic fire unexpectedly billowed out from the island toward the sea and *Liberator* did Donovan decide to give the order to submerge and by then it was too late. All he could do was watch helplessly as the flame wall came closer and closer and images of being charred to the bone raced through his mind. He heard Percy's intake of breath, and he braced for the wave of heat.

One hundred yards from *Liberator*, the fiery mass lost its momentum. Where it made contact with the sea, the water bubbled and boiled and sent up vaporous clouds of steam. Then, as quickly as it appeared, the blanket of flame disappeared, shriveling and contracting upon itself, consuming its own energy. All that remained were tendrils of steam and smoke and the churning sea.

"That was too close for comfort," Percy remarked.

Donovan scanned the island, his features hardening at the sight of the ravaged, burnt wasteland that now existed in place of a luxuriant paradise. All the trees, brush, and flowers were gone. All the birds and the insects. And all the natives.

Thunder boomed and lightning flashed around the rim of the volcano, the result of the friction caused by the column of steam striking the crater walls. Chunks of flaming magma were blasted over the cone and flung thousands of feet. Molten rock began to seep over the rim and through the ruptured side, creeping slowly down the volcano. Glowing globes of flame were launched skyward.

A hand rested on Donovan's left shoulder and he turned to find Alex, her visage a study in sorrow.

"In their own way, they were basically decent people."

"I know."

"I wish there was something we could have done."

"So do I."

Muffled explosions sounded from the volcano, and fiery missiles the size of tanks were expelled from the crater to crash onto the island at scattered locations.

"Let's take her down, Mr. Percy," Donovan directed.

"Aye, Captain."

The obliteration of the Nuranus had a chilling, sobering effect on the crew of *Liberator*. Despite the initial violence, most of the crewmen had been elated to discover a small population of healthy, normal people. In the States the pathological white-shirts were everywhere, and the few pockets of sane survivors were few and far between. After the widespread destruction wrought by the nuclear holocaust, finding anyone who had survived was a cause for celebration. To have traveled so far, 4,400 miles from San Francisco to the Marshalls, and then to have the first islanders they met exterminated by an Armageddon-induced catastrophe, made every member of the crew realize that no matter how much distance they covered, or how much time elapsed, they would never be free from the consequences of World War Three.

Seated in his swivel chair on the bridge the next morning, Donovan stared absently at the Cyclops display as the screen depicted a range of guyots, flat-topped seamounts, on the ocean floor. "Our heading, Mr. Hooper?" he inquired idly.

"One-seven-zero, Captain."

"Steady as she goes at half speed."

"Yes, sir."

Donovan glanced at the communications officer. "Mr. Jennings, are you still being bothered by that glitch?"

"No, Captain. Haven't had a false contact all morning."

"And still no sign at all of *Nemesis?*"

"None."

Executive Officer Percy strolled over to the chair. "Are we going to put in at every island in the Marshalls, Captain?"

"No. From here on out, we'll only send a landing party to those islands where habitation is indicated. And if we find one suitable as a port, we'll check it over carefully. For now, we'll make a sweep of the eastern Marshall chain, the Radak. If we don't find what we're after, then we'll check out the western group."

"And if we don't locate a site there?"

"Then it's on to the Gilbert Islands. There has to be an island somewhere in the South Pacific we can use."

"Just so there isn't a volcano on it," Percy said.

"We'll steer clear of all volcanoes," Donovan assured him.

"I remember reading somewhere that there are over a dozen volcanoes on Russia's Kamchatka Peninsula," Percy mentioned. "I hope every damn one is active now."

"You really won't be satisfied until you have a chance to take revenge on the Russians, will you?"

"No, sir."

"Even knowing they might not have started the war?"

"Maybe you're right, Captain. Maybe the Russians didn't punch their buttons first. But it doesn't matter. The Commies threw everything they had at us. Our country, for all intents and purposes, is

131

gone, and all the ones we love the most have been killed. So even if I buy the story that the Soviets weren't the instigators, they're as much to blame as whoever did set the war in motion."

"Well, if there are any Russians left, I hope they don't feel the same way you do."

Captain First Rank Ivan Vazov stared morosely at the cup of black coffee on the table in front of him, his visage twisted by a scowl, thinking of Ludmila and his two boys. He'd dreamed of them again last night, dreamed of them being vaporized by a nuclear missile, and the horrifyingly vivid vision had snapped him from his slumber to sit bolt upright in his bunk, his body caked with a clammy sweat. The nights were the worst, he thought. Asleep he had no control over his thoughts, and the painful memories flooded into his consciousness unbidden. No wonder he was having trouble sleeping.

"May I join you, Comrade Captain?"

Vazov looked up and smiled at his protégé, Executive Officer Dragominov. "Of course, Nikolai. Take a seat."

The junior officer sat down, a cup of coffee in his right hand. "Thank you, Captain."

"Please, Nikolai. We're in the galley. We're friends. You may dispense with the formality."

"Yes, sir."

"We haven't enjoyed a good talk in ages," Vazov noted.

"No, Comrade Captain. And there is something I must talk to you about," Dragominov said, and glanced around to insure they were out of earshot.

"What is it?"

"Our revered political officer."

"What has that bastard done now?" Vazov snapped.

"Comrade Vatutin called me into his cabin for a chat," Dragominov disclosed.

Vazov took a sip of coffee, hoping to disguise his feelings toward the political officer. If the simpleton didn't stop meddling in affairs that didn't concern him, Vazov might be tempted to end Serge Vatutin's deleterious influence once and for all. "What about?" he asked calmly.

"About you. About your decision to follow the American sub and monitor her actions instead of blowing her out of the water."

"I have explained my reason to him repeatedly," Vazov said, and sighed. "It is impossible to get through to that man. He sees and hears only what he wants."

"He wants us to blow up the American submarine."

"What did he say to you?"

"Comrade Vatutin knows we are very close friends. He was hoping he could persuade me to have a word with you, to influence you to change your mind."

Anger blazed from Vazov's eyes. He put the cup down and rested his hands in his lap so the young officer couldn't see them, then clenched his fists until his knuckles hurt.

"From what I understand," Dragonimov went on, "he has taken other officers aside to prevail upon them to do the same. His desire to crush the Americans is driving him over the brink, I fear."

"Vatutin went over the brink a long time ago," Vazov muttered. "The man has no sense of proportion, no common sense, period. All he wants is vengeance, vengeance, vengeance."

Dragominov studied his superior for several seconds. "And you, Comrade Captain? How do you feel?"

"I will abide by my earlier decision. We will wait

133

and see if the *Liberator* conducts us to other American ships, and then we will sink them all."

"Yes, sir."

Vazov detected a subtle nuance in the executive officer's voice. "Does that bother you, Nikolai?"

"May I be totally honest?"

"I wouldn't have it any other way."

"Yes, Captain. It bothers me. We have received no communications from the Motherland since the war. For all we know, one side or the other might have capitulated or there might be a truce in effect, provided both governments somehow survived. Destroying the Americans seems like such a waste."

"If anyone else spoke this way, I would brand them as a coward," Vazov commented. "But you're no coward, my young friend. Even if what you say was true, we would still have our duty to perform. And our duty, as far as we are concerned, is to destroy enemy ships."

"But what if—" Dragominov began, then caught himself, leery of voicing his innermost thoughts for fear of coming across as unpatriotic.

"Go on. Finish what you were going to say."

Dragominov hesitated for just a moment. His trust of Vazov prompted him to continue. "But what if there are no other ships that have survived the war, whether ours or theirs? What if there are only a few warships remaining on both sides? Do we keep fighting until every last one of us has been exterminated? Do we wipe ourselves off the face of the Earth? Where does the madness end, Comrade?"

"The madness never ends," Vazov responded immediately. "From the cradle to the grave, life is a lesson in lunacy." He paused. "When I was much younger, Nikolai, I used to think about such things. I would wonder why the Americans hated us so much, and why we couldn't live in peace. I wondered why there was so much needless suffering, and why everyone always seemed to be out to get the other fellow."

"And?"

"And I decided the world was a crazy place in which to live. The best we can hope for is to live to a ripe old age and die while sleeping in our bed," Vazov said, and his mouth curled in a wry smile. "At least, that was the best we could hope for before the madness reached its inevitable conclusion. Now all we can do is take life a day at a time and hope we live to see the morning sun."

"Surely there is more to life than that, Captain?"

"For a while I believed there was meaning to our lives. But that all ended when my family was killed. Karl Marx was right all along, Nikolai. There is no God. How could there be? What kind of Deity would allow such madness to exist?"

Dragominov had no answer to that one. He sat back and swallowed some coffee.

"So you see, my young friend," Vazov resumed, "we are locked into our destiny. We must follow this madness to its conclusion. We were trained to seek out and destroy enemy shipping, and that is exactly what we will do. When the time comes, Comrade Vatutin will get his wish. We will sink the American sub and send all of her hands to the bottom."

"With all due respect, Comrade Captain, I still think it is such a waste."

Two hours later Donovan stood on the topside bridge, breathing in the salty, moist Pacific air, and surveyed the horizon. Far to the south a column of blackish gray smoke wafted high into the atmosphere.

"Another damn volcano, you think?" Charlie asked.

"We'll soon know."

"Didn't Matal tell us that other clans lived in this vicinity?"

"Yeah," Donovan replied.

Charlie nodded at the smoke. "The way our luck has been running, that was probably their island."

Donovan looked to his right and stiffened. Several distinctive fins were knifing the water less than fifty yards from the ship. Sharks again. Lots of them. Was it his imagination, or were there more of the things than usual? He watched a particularly huge fin wind slowly to the south, as if the fish was pacing the sub.

Charlie had noticed them, too. "If we had enough ammo to spare, I'd use those sharks for target practice."

"You don't like them either?"

"Nope. A buddy of mine was in a chopper that developed a stabilizer problem and had to ditch in the Sea of Japan. There were three others on board with him. They managed to get their life raft afloat and their emergency locator beacon operational," Pirate related. "The weather turned a bit rough. Lots of clouds and high waves. And then the shark came."

"Just one?"

Charlie nodded. "They never did figure out exactly what kind of shark it was. A great white, maybe. Anyway, the damn thing tore into their life raft. Actually ruptured the seams and it started to sink. They used their shark repellent, but that junk doesn't work." He paused, his features clouding. "They hung on to the raft for dear life, trying to stay as still as possible so they wouldn't attract the shark. It didn't do them any good."

"How many did the shark get?"

"The only one who lived was my buddy. If another chopper hadn't arrived and hauled his butt from the drink, that shark would have added him to its list."

Donovan could imagine the horror of floating in the water, defenseless and vulnerable, never knowing when razor-sharp teeth might tear into a dangling leg, and he shook his head to clear his mind.

Just then Percy's voice crackled from the topside bridge speaker. "Captain, multiple contacts. Range eight miles."

15

"Up periscope," Donovan commanded.

"Raising periscope."

"What can you tell me, Mr. Jennings?" Donovan inquired of his communications officer.

"There are seventeen contacts, Captain. No heat generation, so they must be using sails or oars. The length of each is uniform, about twenty feet. They're proceeding on a bearing of two-nine-zero and should cross in front of our bow within twenty minutes."

Donovan glanced at the small icons on the viewscreen, then peered through the periscope. He'd ordered *Liberator* to be brought down to periscope depth as a precaution. Up above, *Liberator* was vulnerable, but hidden under the surface they would have the advantage of surprise unless those seventeen craft possessed sonar, which he doubted. They must be outriggers, he deduced, and in less than a half hour he confirmed his hunch.

The canoes were little more than dots at first, but they gradually grew in resolution as they approached the sub's position. Donovan increased the magnification factor and established that each outrigger was crammed with islanders. Men, women, and children had been packed into the canoes like sardines in a tin can. Four of the outriggers also carried piles of provisions. The men were paddling at a steady rate to the northwest.

"Mr. Percy, what do you make of this?" Donovan queried, and stepped aside so his executive officer could use the periscope.

Percy took one look and provided his assessment. "I'd say a whole village is on the move."

"That's what I thought," Donovan concurred, and stared at the helmsman. "Mr. Hooper, take us up. Easy does it. Get within hailing distance of those natives."

"Aye, Captain."

"What do you have in mind, sir?" Percy questioned.

"We'll see if any of them speak English and find out where they're heading."

"Do you want a security squad?"

"Negative. The sight of armed men would only panic the natives. Just you and I will go."

"Yes, sir."

"Down 'scope," Donovan directed, and waited while his instructions were carried out. The fact that another clan had survived the war increased his confidence in being able to find a habitable base of operations. From an environmental standpoint alone, coming to the South Pacific had turned out to be a wise idea. His long-term plan called for *Liberator* to range far and wide in search of other survivors, and a base in the Marshalls, or even the Gilbert Islands or the Society Islands, would put Australia, Indonesia, eastern Asia, and the western coasts of the United States and South America within easy reach.

"Ready when you are, Captain," Percy said.

Moments later Donovan stood on the topside bridge and scrutinized the outriggers. The natives had stopped paddling, and many gawked in consternation at the sub. Others, more hostile, scowled

139

and waved their weapons. He activated the hailing system. "This is Captain Thomas Donovan of the U.S.S. *Liberator*. Do you understand me? Is there anyone who can speak English?"

None of the natives responded.

"I repeat. I'm Captain Donovan, and I would like to talk to you. Where are you headed? Where are you from? What is the name of your tribe?"

A sinewy man seated in the bow of the foremost canoe leaned on the gunwale and cupped his right hand to his mouth. "Go away! Leave us alone!"

"Who are you? Where are you from?"

"We want nothing to do with you!"

Donovan exchanged a puzzled glance with Percy, then faced the islanders. "We won't hurt you. We want to help, if we can. Where are you from?"

The native pointed to the southeast. "Two days from here."

"Where are you going?"

"To find a new home."

"Why did you leave your old one?"

Again the native pointed, only this time at the column of smoke to the south. "One of those destroyed our village."

The news disturbed Donovan. This meant that two volcanoes had recently erupted along the Radak chain, counting the one last night, which did not bode well for the prospects of discovering a safe haven. "We can help you, if you wish," he offered.

"No."

"Why not?"

"We don't want your help."

"What harm can it do?"

"No!" the native reiterated angrily. "We know of the war. You have already done enough!"

"But we weren't involved in the conflict."

"Save your lies for someone who will believe you."

140

Percy shook his head. "It's no use, Captain. Why waste your breath?"

Ignoring the comment, Donovan tried one last time. "Is there anything you need? We have a doctor on board if anyone requires medical attention."

"All we want is to be left in peace," the native declared, and motioned with his right arm. The canoes resumed their course to the northwest, the islanders glaring at the ship in undisguised hatred.

"So much for that idea," Percy remarked.

"We had to try. Wherever we find survivors, we have to do whatever we can to assist them."

"There's not much we can do if they don't want our help, sir," Percy noted.

"More's the pity," Donovan said, not surprised in the least by the younger man's cynicism. He knew that Percy would rather be seeking out enemy vessels than acting as a Good Samaritan. Barely thirty years old, Percy had acquired a widespread reputation as a chronic hothead and had been passed over for command several times by COMSUBPAC. Although Percy excelled at war games, the Navy brass had decided he didn't possess the seasoned temperament a submarine commander should have.

"Look at that, Captain," the firebrand stated, gazing at the smoke.

Donovan looked up and saw the top of the volcano come into view, lava spilling down its sides. Gradually an island materialized, a barren atoll crisscrossed by rivers of molten magma, devoid of all life. At least there, he thought with satisfaction, the eruption hadn't resulted in any loss of human lives. The extensive volcanism in the Marshalls was beginning to worry him. Even though he had anticipated such would be the case, and even though the computer projections all had substantiated the hypothesis, the degree of volcanism went way beyond his earlier expectations. If the pattern continued to hold, then the prospect of finding additional native villages intact was slim. The Nuranus had lived on an island situated on the extreme northeast fringe of the Marshalls. If the volcanic activity was spreading northward from the more unstable region near New Zealand, then the volcano on the Nuranu island had been one of the last to flare to life in the Marshalls. The insight sobered him. He stared at the flowing lava, troubled, and asked himself a critical question: Is this all we're going to find?

It was.

For two days *Liberator* prowled southward along the eastern chain, discovering over a dozen active volcanoes in the process. Nowhere did they locate an inhabited village, although twice they passed deserted indigenous settlements where not even a mongrel dog stirred. None of the islands was ideal for use as a sub port, so Donovan did not bother to send landing parties ashore.

Alex and Peter took atmospheric readings at regular intervals and reported that the radiation levels in the Marshalls were barely above normal. The volcanic ash in the atmosphere, however, was another story. Minute particulate matter disgorged into the air created massive, sooty clouds that occasionally covered the sky from horizon to horizon. Most of the ash was borne to the east by the prevailing trade winds, although islands and atolls within the immediate vicinity of a volcano were frequently covered by a grayish white film.

Communications Officer Jennings kept the ship's radio receivers scanning all known frequencies, but only static filled the electromagnetic spectrum. No radio broadcasts were detected, not even on the shortwave band. The Cray-9 computer handled the listening chores automatically, searching the multitude of frequencies that had been programmed into it by top naval experts.

By the time the ship reached the last cluster of islands in the Radak chain, the mood on *Liberator* had changed from optimism to skepticism. Many crew members began to believe that encountering the Nuranus and the second tribe had been flukes, and a subcurrent of discontent surfaced. Several openly voiced their contention that searching the Marshalls was a waste of precious days better spent engaged in determining how extensively America had been devastated by the war.

Donovan spent hours at a stretch on the topside bridge with Percy, Jennings, and Helmsman Hooper. He constantly scoured the sea with binoculars, hoping against hope that the next atoll or island would be the one they needed. Again and again he experienced disappointment. After the sub completed its sweep of the Sunrise chain, he toyed with the notion of heading for the States but changed his mind. His gut instinct told him to press on, so press on he did.

Liberator swung to the west and in 130 miles came to the western chain, the Ralik, or Sunset, group. Bearing to the north, the sub continued hunting for a permanent berthing place. Hope flared among the crew as the ship neared Kwajalein, the world's largest atoll and the site of a U.S.-operated airport prior to Armageddon.

American forces first landed on Kwajalein during World War Two, wresting control from the Japanese in 1944. After capturing the atoll, the United States used it as a Navy base and later converted it to an airport. With over ninety islands embraced in the atoll, a total land area of six square miles, and with a population of 4,118 before the missiles flew, Kwajalein ranked as one of the more prominent centers in the Marshalls.

Percy, whose eyesight was exceptional, spotted the smoke first. "Captain, Kwajalein is burning," he announced.

A few seconds later Donovan spied the smoke, too, and his brow knit as he considered the eight thin ribbons spiraling toward the clouds. "Those are from fires, not a volcano. Mr. Hooper, take us in. Mr. Percy, I want additional lookouts and a weapons party on the bridge in two minutes."

Liberator drew closer to land and a town became visible near the shore. The smoke rose from different locations, including a blazing yacht at anchor close to the dock. No one moved on the beach or in the streets, and an eery silence prevailed.

Charlie emerged from the hatch, took one look, and commented, "This is spooky. It reminds me of Seattle and San Francisco." He hefted the Luigi Franchi in his left hand. "Will we go check it out?"

"We will not," Donovan responded.

"Think it's white-shirts again?"

"Whether it's white-shirts, looters, or pirates is irrelevant. The airport is obviously out of commission. The town was either evacuated or abandoned, and I doubt there's anyone around we'd want to contact."

"There's somebody around," Percy interjected.

Donovan heard the distant laughter and gazed at the beach, where a group of nine or ten men had appeared. They were clearly enjoying themselves, carousing merrily, and several were even singing.

"They must be drunk," Charlie said.

"They're looters, I'll bet," Percy remarked.

Shouts of surprise came from the group as one of their number saw the submarine, followed by strident oaths and exclamations. Rifles were waved overhead, and a shot cracked across the waves.

"Those dummies can't hit us from there," Charlie declared.

144

"We could move in closer and let our weapons party take care of them," Percy suggested.

"We'll head northward," Donovan said.

"It would be easy to round them up, Captain."

"I'm not about to needlessly risk lives to satisfy our curiosity. We'll carry on with our search."

"Yes, sir."

Once again *Liberator* sailed northward, passing a series of small islands. None appeared to be inhabited or would suffice as a base. Hooper plotted a course to the northwest at Donovan's command, and the next day, late in the afternoon, they approached a large, isolated atoll in the northwestern corner of the Marshalls, a historic cluster of forty sandy islets with a meager land area of two and a quarter miles. Historic because the atoll was known as Eniwetok, which had served as a proving ground for the United States Atomic Energy Commission in the 1940s and 1950s. Three atomic bombs were exploded at Eniwetok in 1948 and four more in 1951. Then, in 1952, the site was used to test the world's first thermonuclear device—the H-bomb.

Donovan stared at the serene setting, where gulls and other birds frolicked or dived for fish, and contemplated the irony of Eniwetok, the testing ground where the atomic age began in earnest, the very age that would result in mankind's near destruction, being untouched by the war.

From Eniwetok *Liberator* bore to the east, and in due course passed another famous atoll, one every naval officer learned about at the Academy, namely Bikini. Consisting of thirty-six islets located on a crescent-shaped reef some twenty-five miles in length, Bikini Atoll had also been used for atomic and hydrogen bomb testing. The United States had gone so far as to remove the native population to another island so it could use Bikini.

Donovan recalled reading about one such test in

particular because of the loss of several ships deliberately positioned within the blast radius. The first underwater test of an atomic bomb had destroyed a flotilla of abandoned warships, including the battleship *Arizona* and four submerged submarines. The equivalent of 50,000 tons of TNT had crushed them as if they were made of soft putty instead of tempered steel.

And now there Bikini Atoll sat, untouched like its cousin, the site where mass annihilation had been perfected to a fine art, unscathed by the nuclear tempest it helped spawn.

With the circuit of the Marshall Islands completed, Donovan ordered a new course to be set for the Gilbert Islands. No sooner had he given the command than Communications Officer Jennings spoke up.

"Captain, I'm having problems with that glitch again."

"It figures," Donovan muttered. "What else can go wrong?"

16

Captain First Rank Ivan Vazov stood behind the communications operator's chair, his brawny hands clasped in the curve of his spine, and frowned. "There have been no transmissions whatsoever?"

"None, Captain," the warrant officer responded.

"They have not sent a single message?"

"No, sir. Not since the ship-to-shore exchange during the eruption of the volcano."

"And they have not received any transmissions?"

"None."

"And you have checked every frequency the Americans use?"

"Yes, Captain. We are automatically checking every frequency. No other ship has contacted them, nor have they been in touch with any land facility."

Vazov straightened and slowly lowered his arms to his sides. He turned to find Dragominov two meters away, watching him. "Well, Nikolai, it appears the Americans are not going to make contact with other warships. Their behavior is most inexplicable. If I didn't know better, I'd swear they were taking a cruise of the South Pacific."

Dragominov grinned. "They must be searching for something, Captain."

"But what? Why did they make a complete circuit of the Marshall Islands?"

"I could not hazard a guess, Comrade Captain."

"And now they are less than twelve hours from the Gilberts," Vazov mentioned thoughtfully, his tone conveying his perplexity. He sighed and gazed at the SHADOW operator. "SHADOW status?"

"All systems are fully functional, Comrade Captain. The Vostoy is concealing us from their sensors."

"Perfect," Vazov said, and made the decision he had been putting off for days. "Nikolai, I want to speak to the crew. The entire crew. Open the ship-wide link."

"Yes, Captain."

Vazov felt every eye in the control room on him as he cleared his throat and moved to the console to pick up the microphone. They all knew what was coming. Now it was up to him to inspire them to perform their duty diligently. "Comrades, this is your captain speaking," he began, his voice booming from a dozen speakers situated throughout the sub.

Political Officer Vatutin entered the control room and stared expectantly at Vazov.

"Comrades, the moment you have been waiting for is at hand. We are going to attack and sink the American ship *Liberator*," Vazov stated, then paused for effect, to have them hanging on his next words. "This task will not be easy, but is is a task we *must* achieve. All of us have lost loved ones because of the imperialists. There isn't a man on board who hasn't felt sorrow because of the Americans, who attacked our Motherland without warning, killing millions upon millions of our countrymen before our poor comrades knew what hit them. Our Motherland is no more. All of our attempts to contact our homeland have met with

148

failure because there is virtually no one there to contact."

Vatutin nodded vigorously, pleased at the speech.

"How can we allow the loss of our loved ones to go unpunished?" Vazov went on, his tone becoming gruff. "How can we let the Americans get away with what they have done? We can't! Not if we are men! Not if we are Russian sailors! Not if our devotion to the Motherland and our love for our families and friends is more than mere lip service! We can't!"

"Yes!" Vatutin whispered. "Yes, Comrade Captain!"

"If we want to be able to hold our heads high, to have any shred of pride and self-respect, we must take retribution for the catastrophe inflicted on the Motherland by the imperialists. We must send the *Liberator* to the bottom of the sea."

Listening attentively, Nikolai Dragominov happened to glance at the political officer and was shocked to see a mad gleam in Vatutin's eyes.

"Now I will tell you about the nature of our enemy," Vazov was saying. "The *Liberator* is the newest submarine in the American fleet. Soviet Naval Intelligence reported that the ship is the most sophisticated vessel the Americans have, and we all know what that means. It is no secret the Americans have long enjoyed an edge in technology, only because they took so many German scientists under their wing at the end of World War Two. So we can expect this *Liberator* to be the ultimate in American naval power."

Vatutin saw the executive officer watching him and smiled.

"But there is one fact all of us must keep in mind. The *Charkov* is the ultimate in Soviet naval power. Our ship is the equal of any the Americans ever built. This *Liberator* may be formidable, but so is

149

the *Charkov.* We go into this battle with an even chance of victory. A better than even chance, since we are in the right."

Dragominov glanced at his mentor.

"Yes, Comrades! We are in the right!" Vazov re-iterated. "We are avenging the sneak attack on our Motherland and the deaths of our loved ones. We are paying the imperialists back, in a small measure, for their infamy. And once we have disposed of the *Liberator,* we will seek out other American vessels and do the same to them. We shall become the avenging scourge of the high seas. Those Americans who still live shall tremble when they hear about us."

Was Ivan serious? Dragominov wondered, and gazed around him, surprised at the credulous, receptive expressions on his fellows.

"And now a word of caution, Comrades," Vazov said. "The Americans are all professionals. They train their crews extensively. To defeat them, we must keep our wits about us. We must be as crafty as the fox in the henhouse, as patient as the Siberian tiger waiting for game to come within charging range, and as quick as a cobra when the time to strike arrives." He coughed lightly. "Each of you must attend to his post with the utmost care. There will be no margin for mistakes. Perform your duty as best as you know how, and victory is assured."

In his enthusiam, Political Officer Vatutin forgot himself and cried, "To victory, Comrades!"

Vazov looked up, then nodded. "You heard our revered political officer. He has the right attitude. We must believe that we will win, and we *will* win. Keep your loved ones in mind and you will be surprised at your resolve. Follow my orders explicitly and by the end of this day the American sub will be resting on the ocean bed. That is all." He replaced the microphone and turned.

"Well done, Comrade," Vatutin declared. He walked over and patted Vazov on the shoulder. "I couldn't have said it any better myself. If I had any doubts about your devotion, they are all erased."

"Thank you, Serge," Vazov responded dryly.

"I can't wait until we have blown them to pieces."

"You must restrain your emotions, Comrade. It will be a while before we are in a position to fire a torpedo."

Vatutin blinked a few times. "But I thought you said we would be attacking soon."

A soft sigh hissed from Vazov's lips. "Patience, Comrade. Patience. We are presently about eighteen kilometers from the American ship. If we were to fire a torpedo from this range, it is doubtful we would score a hit. There are too many tricks a wise sub commander can employ to evade a torpedo."

"What kind of tricks?"

"A torpedo can be outwitted, Comrade. The homing sensors can be jammed. Or the American commander could take evasive action. Even guided torpedoes can be deceived. If a target is on or near the surface, the sonar pulses guiding the torpedo can be reflected and the torpedo will miss. Or the Americans can fire a decoy, a torpedo of their own that will transmit signals to our torpedo and convince it that their torpedo is actually their sub. Do you understand?"

"I think so."

"Then you can appreciate why we will not fire until we are much, much closer."

"But surely they'll detect us."

"No, Comrade. The Vostoy veiling device prevents their sensors from registering our presence. And our SHADOW stalking system will enable us to creep up on them and fire at such close range they will be unable to avoid our torpedo."

151

Vatutin pondered for a moment. "How close must we be?"

"A range of five thousand meters would be ideal, but in this instance I want to get much closer."

"How close?"

"Three thousand meters at the very minimum."

The idea of being in such proximity to the American sub seemed to bother the political officer. "We will be breathing down their necks, figuratively speaking."

"Exactly. They will have little time to react. Our chances of success are much greater the closer we can get," Vazov said. "If I thought it would be safe, I would try to get even closer than three thousand meters."

"Why wouldn't it be safe?"

"Because the Americans use incredibly sensitive devices on their ships. Even with the Vostoy in operation, they might be able to detect us if we approach nearer than three thousand meters."

A thought made Vatutin smile. "But we have the element of surprise on our side, Comrade Captain."

"That we do. And the element of surprise has won many a battle, many a war. If all goes as I plan, they won't know we are even in the same ocean until we fire our torpedoes."

"I envy you, Ivan."

"Oh?"

"You will give the order that will send the rotten imperialists to the bottom."

"Every seaman will take part in this victory. I am no better than the sum total of all those who serve under me," Vazov said.

"You are too modest," Vatutin replied, and surveyed the control room. "I liked what you said about becoming the avenging scourge of the high seas. The role suits us. We will make the Americans pay dearly for their perfidy."

For once Vazov agreed wholeheartedly with the political officer. "That we will," he concurred, and moved over to Dragominov. "What did you think of my speech, Nikolai?"

"You certainly have the crew fired up, Captain."

"And what about you? I noticed the way you looked at me when I mentioned being in the right."

"With all due respect, Captain, are we?"

Vazov checked to ensure that none of the seamen were listening to their conversation. "Do you have your doubts?"

"I honestly don't know anymore, sir."

"Then keep your feelings to yourself. I don't want doubt to infect our crew. We must be strong if we are to persevere."

"Yes, Captain."

"And as for the matter of being in the right, I am disappointed that you would have any reservations. I don't. Every time I think of Ludmila and my sons, I know I'm doing what must be done."

"I'm sorry, sir. I will never question you again."

"Please, Nikolai. Don't patronize me. Your integrity is one of your strong points. If I want unquestioning patriotism, I always have Vatutin."

Dragominov smiled sheepishly. "Then I shall continue to voice my objections as I see fit, Comrade."

Vazov moved to the middle of the control room, his eyes roving over his men and the banks of equipment. "Sonar Operator, what is the status of our target?"

"The American sub is at a depth of nine hundred and twenty-three meters, moving at forty knots on a bearing of one-seven-eight."

"Range?"

"Seventeen kilometers, Captain."

"Executive Officer Dragominov, sound battle stations," Vazov ordered, and listened to the strident hoots of the alarm that blared in every compartment on the *Charkov*. In less than a minute his protégé spoke the words he wanted to hear.

"All men are at battle stations, Comrade Captain."

"SHADOW Operator, confirm system is at peak performance."

"Confirmed, Captain. The Vostoy also."

"Excellent. Then we shall proceed at forty-five knots. Silent running," Vazov directed.

"Silent running," Dragominov repeated. Now the game of cat and mouse began in earnest, he thought. Even though the Vostoy could hide the *Charkov* from American sonar, as their vessel drew nearer to the American sub any exceptionally loud noise on board might be detected. The men would now speak softly. Any activity that could produce unwanted noise, such as cooking, was banned. Cold sandwiches would suffice until the captain canceled the order.

Vazov glanced at the sonar operator. "Sonar, you will monitor the *Liberator* on all passive systems only. Is that understood?"

"Passive only. Yes, Comrade Captain."

"If they turn their active sonar on us, even if it is for just one ping, I want to know immediately."

"Of course, Captain."

Vazov nodded and grinned. A thrill ran through him at the prospect of avenging his family. And, too, he looked forward to putting the *Charkov* to the supreme test. "Helmsman, you will be prepared to take over manual operation from the SHADOW system at my command."

"Yes, sir," Kuprevici responded.

"Executive Officer Dragominov, you will verify the torpedo room has four torpedoes primed for firing."

"Torpedo room reports four Tigerfish ready to fire, Captain."

154

"Good. Four should be more than enough if we can get as close as I want," Vazov mentioned. "Sonar Operator, you will read off the range in five-hundred-meter increments starting at fifteen thousand meters."

"Yes, Comrade Captain."

Vazov rubbed his hands together and chuckled. "The Americans can count the time they have left on this Earth in hours."

17

Donovan was seated in his swivel chair on the bridge, mulling his options, when Alex appeared. She came directly toward him and placed her hand on his right forearm. "So here you are. Did you get tired of all that fresh air?"

"We can't stay on the surface all the time. It's too dangerous."

"That's not what I meant and you know it," Alex said, studying the set of his countenance. "What's troubling you?"

"Nothing."

She leaned down and whispered, "You can lie to me after last night?" A grin creased her lips. "You must be coldhearted as sin."

Donovan warmed to her sincere affection. He shook his head and gazed absently at the Cyclops. "Sorry. I'm beginning to wonder if we're doing the right thing."

"Searching for a base in the South Pacific?"

"We're expending a lot of time on this project, time better spent hunting for survivors we can help."

"Hey, aren't you the one who insisted that finding a base is our paramount concern?"

"Yeah, but—"

" 'Essential' was the word you used, as I recall.

Well, if having a base is so damned important, you can't give up now. I never figured you for a quitter, Donovan."

"Thanks. But other factors have entered the picture."

"Like what?"

"Like the widespread volcanic activity."

"The Cray-9 projected the possibility."

"I know," Donovan said. "But I didn't quite expect it to be as bad as it is."

"So the volcanism in the Marshalls was worse than we anticipated. So what? We've checked one measly island chain. There are dozens more out there, and any one of them could include an island ideal for your purposes. There's the Gilberts, Samoa, and the Society Islands, just to mention three."

"I know."

"Then there's the Fiji Islands, the Caroline Islands, the Mariana Islands, and the Line Islands. Not to mention the Solomon Islands, the New Hebrides, the—"

Now it was Donovan's turn to interrupt her. "I get the point. I've read the list the computer put out. But there are so many damn islands in the South Pacific, we could search for years."

"Surely it won't take that long," Alex commented.

"I hope not," Donovan stated, and pursed his lips. "You've studied the communities in Micronesia and Polynesia. What can we expect in the Gilberts?"

"I'll warn you in advance that they might not have what you want. The Gilberts are a group of sixteen coral reef islands. They're very low, only about twenty feet above sea level on the average, and not one of them has a river or a mountain."

"Terrific."

"There's hope yet. I still think the Society Islands will be our best bet, and they're not all that far from the Gilberts."

"Then we'll head for the Society Islands as soon as we're finished with our sweep of the Gilberts," Donovan proposed.

"Tahiti is located in the Society Islands," Alex mentioned.

"Really?" Donovan leaned back and grinned. "All those beautiful native women dressed in grass skirts. The mind boggles."

Alex pretended to glower. "If I catch your weed eater anywhere near a grass skirt, you're history, mister."

"Is that a threat?"

"A promise."

"Captain," Communications Officer Jennings abruptly spoke up. "The systems repair boys still aren't doing their job right."

"Let me guess," Donovan responded flatly. "You're still registering false contacts."

"Yes, sir. I just had one a minute ago, but when I double-checked there was nothing there. Range nine miles at two-nine-six."

"A bug in your sensors?" Alex inquired.

"We've been having a minor problem for days."

"Anything I can put the computers to work on?"

"Flaze and his crew have been working on it and they can't seem to find the cause. Periodically we're picking up bogus targets."

"And you're sure they're bogus?"

"Sure I'm sure."

"It couldn't be *Nemesis?*"

"If it was, they would have to be using a device that can completely conceal them from our sensors. No such technology exists."

"A device that could make them invisible, you mean?"

"Yeah."

"Like the Domino 3000?"

Donovan straightened. "The what?"

Alex shook her head and snickered. "First the white noise generator and now the Domino 3000. How *do* you Navy types keep abreast of the latest technology? By reading comic books?"

"What about this Domino device?" Donovan inquired, bothered by her reference to the white noise generator, the bioacoustic dampening device *Nemesis* apparently utilized to cover up her screw signature and other machine noises. But even when *Nemesis* used the generator, *Liberator*'s sensors were always able to register *Nemesis* as a distinct target, not a vague, fuzzy echo.

"I read about the Domino 3000 in a journal published by M.I.T.," Alex revealed. "Their school of science was working on a device that would nullify all emissions in the electromagnetic spectrum."

"Nullify how?"

"By projecting a camouflaging electromagnetic barrier or screen that would bend rather than deflect a sound wave, a radio wave, or any other type of emission. The theory was that the Domino 3000 would render the user invisible from conventional detection systems such as sonar and radar."

The revelation troubled Donovan immensely. He sat forward and glanced at Jennings, then back at Alex. "Did they build one of these devices?"

"Not as far as I know. The project never got further than the drawing board."

"Why?"

"Theoretically the concept was sound, but they couldn't formulate a practical means of projecting the electromagentic screen. The last I heard, they were still working on the project but they rated their chances of success as slim."

"So no one ever actually built such a device?"

"Not as far as I know, no," Alex answered. "But

159

the journal article I saw was published about five years ago. Someone might have made a breakthrough and I didn't hear about it."

"I hope not."

"Why? Are you thinking that *Nemesis* might possess such a device?"

"There's always the possibility," Donovan said uncertainly. "But if she does, why hasn't she demonstrated the capability before? She's been able to mask her noise, but not conceal herself from our sensors. This device, if there is one functional, would do the opposite, would conceal the ship but not mask the noise."

"Well, I'd better leave you to your problem," Alex stated. "I'll be working with Peter in the sick bay if you need me."

"Thanks, Alex," Donovan said, and watched her depart, thankful for the wealth of knowledge she carried in her pretty, astute head. Her familiarity with the latest technological developments had proven invaluable against *Nemesis*. Now what was he to make of this Domino business? "Mr. Jennings?"

"Yes, Captain?"

"Check that last false contact again. Active sonar, maximum power, directional signal."

"Checking, sir."

"Comrade Captain, the Americans are pinging with their active sonar."

Vazov stiffened and glanced at the sonar operator. "Are they pinging us?"

"No, Captain. They have directed their signal astern approximately five hundred meters."

"They know we are here," Dragominov declared.

"They can't know!" Vazov replied. "They can't. Not while the Vostoy is veiling the ship."

"Then why did they ping our previous position, Captain?"

Vazov pondered for a moment, scratching his chin. "They must be guessing. Perhaps they detected a faint echo."

"Should we dive deeper, sir?" Dragominov asked.

"No. We continue as planned. The SHADOW will duplicate all of their maneuvers. We don't dive deeper unless they do."

"Comrade Captain, the Americans have stopped pinging," the sonar operator reported.

"See?" Vazov said, and grinned. "We have nothing to worry about."

"Negative reading now, sir," Communications Officer Jennings stated.

Percy approached the captain's chair. "Do you really think there's something out there?"

"Could be," Donovan responded, and rested his chin in his right hand.

"But that glitch has been annoying us for days, sir. If it's legit, if there's a ship out there, why haven't they attacked? Why have they been trailing us all over the South Pacific?"

"Who knows?" Donovan replied. "First we must verify there is someone trailing us, then we'll speculate on their motive." He looked at Jennings. "Any more weak echoes?"

"None, sir."

Donovan performed a few mental calculations. The last false target had been 15,840 yards away. If there was another vessel—and for the sake of argument he assumed there was one—they might be able to verify the fact by using the laser once the mystery ship came within range. "Mr. Jennings, activate the laser. Probe status. If you hear another weak contact within ten thousand yards, lock the

161

laser on the target and see if we can identify whoever they are."

"Aye, Captain."

Next Donovan turned to the helsman. "Mr.
Hooper, are we still bearing one-seven-eight?"

"Yes, sir."

"Initiate a zigzag pattern from one-six-zero to
one-nine-zero and back again."

"Beginning a zigzag pattern," Hooper replied.

"What good will this do, sir?" Percy inquired.

"Maybe none."

"Then why are we doing it, Captain?"

Donovan smiled. "Humor me, Mr. Percy."

The sonar operator raised his head and cried,
"The Americans are changing course, Comrade
Captain."

Vazov was at the man's side in a second. "What
is their new bearing?"

"One moment, sir." The seaman watched his
monitor, his body tense. "The new bearing is one-
nine-zero."

"Now what are they up to?" Dragominov asked
from behind Vazov.

"Wait, Captain. They are changing course once
again."

"What?"

"Yes, sir. They are swinging back to one-seven-
eight. No, make that one-seven-zero."

"What in Lenin's name are they doing?" Dragominov wondered.

"Now they are at one-six-zero," the sonar operator
informed them.

Vazov folded his arms across his chest and nodded. "This American skipper is a cagey one, yes?
He is playing a game with us."

"What kind of game?" Dragominov queried.

The sonar operator interjected the latest observation. "The *Liberator* is changing course yet again, Comrade Captain. Back to one-nine-zero."

"As I suspected," Vazov said, nodding in satisfaction. "This American, Nikolai, is putting us through our paces. He hopes we will give ourselves away, that all this turning and maneuvering will cause us to make more noise than we would running a straight course."

"But it won't," Dragominov said.

"He doesn't know that." Vazov looked at the sonar operator. "What is the range?"

"Coming up on fourteen kilometers and still closing, Captain."

"Excellent. Let the American play his games. Before he realizes we are here, he will be breathing water."

"Still nothing, Mr. Jennings?"

"Nothing, Captain."

"Okay. Keep me posted," Donovan said, and leaned back, aware of Percy's critical gaze. Maybe he was making the proverbial mountain out of a molehill, but he had learned a long time ago to rely on his gut feelings, and his gut told him something wasn't quite right. He debated whether to surface and decided the action was unwarranted. If another ship was approximately nine miles off to the north, or even a bit closer, that was too far off to spot it visually. The range of visibility from the topside bridge to the horizon came to five and a half or six miles on a clear day. "Mr. Hooper, what's our ETA for the Gilbert Islands?"

"At our current speed, ten hours, sir."

Ten hours. It seemed like an eternity. He chided himself for not paying attention to the glitch sooner, then consoled himself with the fact that *Liberator* was a new ship and new ships were notorious for needing bugs worked out of their systems. Maybe it was a bug, after all, and all that talk about the Domino 3000 had got him worked up over nothing. According to Alex the damn thing had never been built.

Try as he might, though, Donovan couldn't shake a nagging doubt, a sensation of unease. He felt the need for a smoke but shrugged it off. First things first. He had to satisfy himself that *Liberator* wasn't being shadowed. He had to force the other ship to give itself away, to make noise the sensors could locate and identify. And when did any vessel make its most noise? "Mr. Hooper, increase speed to fifty-five knots, course one-eight-zero."

"Yes, sir."

The corners of Donovan's mouth curled upward. A ship made the most noise when it was at top speed. If another vessel lay out there somewhere, they were in for a little surprise.

18

The sonar operator monitored the change first. "Comrade Captain, the Americans are increasing speed."

"Ensure SHADOW duplicates their every move."

"Target is now on a bearing of one-eight-zero at fifty-five knots. We are doing the same."

"Good," Vazov said, his eyes narrowing. The sudden jump in speed did not fool him in the least. Obviously, the American commander hoped a higher speed would cause the *Charkov* to make more noise as the engines strained harder and the twin five-bladed propellers churned the water faster. The bastard. Vazov had expected the American to resume the original course to the Gilbert Islands at cruising speed. Instead, the wily son of a bitch seemed to be intent on verifying the *Charkov*'s presence.

"Is anything wrong, Comrade Captain?" Dragominov inquired. Ever sensitive to his mentor's moods, he perceived that something was troubling his superior.

In a low voice, so none of the crew could overhear, Vazov said softly, "This will not be as easy as I thought it would be."

"We still have the edge. We know exactly where the *Liberator* is, but they have yet to locate us."

"That is what worries me. This American commander will not rest until he is satisfied there is no threat to his ship. And the longer he keeps at it, the more likely it is that we will give ourselves away."

"But the Vostoy is still concealing us from their detection equipment."

"True. But the Vostoy operates most efficiently when we are running at speeds under fifty knots. Now we are at fifty-five and the American will probably go higher."

"So? The Vostoy will still function effectively."

Vazov sighed. "Yes, my young friend. But remember that the Vostoy uses thirty percent of the power our reactors generate. At higher speeds, when so much of our power is being channeled into the Vostoy and our propulsion system simultaneously, there is more likelihood of a brief power fluctuation. If that occurs, the Americans will register our presence for a second or two."

Dragominov shrugged. "But that will not be enough time for them to pinpoint our position."

"Perhaps not. Remember, the *Liberator* is the most advanced sub the Americans ever constructed," Vazov said, and paused. "I just hope they don't go much faster."

"Comrade Captain," the sonar operator reported, "the American ship is now at fifty-seven knots."

"Anything, Mr. Jennings?"

"Negative, sir."

"Mr. Hooper, take us to sixty knots."

"Sixty knots, Captain," the helmsman responded.

Donovan stared at the screen, at the presumably empty expanse of Pacific Ocean, and tried to relax. Engrossed in the Cyclops display, he didn't realize his brother had walked onto the bridge until a friendly hand fell on his left shoulder.

"You look a little tense, Tom."

"Is it that obvious?"

"To me it is."

Donovan nodded at the viewscreen. "Something is out there. I can feel it in my bones."

Pirate chuckled. "I thought I'm supposed to be the one with the intuition."

"Have you ever been in a room with the lights out and you were trying to get from one side to the other?"

"A few times," Charlie replied.

"And how did you get across the room?" Donovan asked, then immediately answered his own question. "You had to feel your way. That's how. And I'll bet that sometimes you just knew an object, a chair or whatever, was right in front of you even though you couldn't see it." He paused. "Well, that's how it is for submarine commanders. We have to feel our way a lot of the time and go by our instincts. And my instincts are telling me that we're not alone. I just wish I had paid attention to them sooner."

Charlie stared at his older brother for a moment, than at the screen. "But there's nothing on the magic screen."

"The what?"

"The Cyclops. Why isn't there a target?"

"I think the other guy is using something that makes him invisible."

"I didn't know such a device existed."

"As far as we know, it doesn't," Donovan said.

"Hmmm," was all Charlie responded.

"Any targets yet, Mr. Jennings?" Donovan inquired.

"None, Captain," the communications officer replied.

"Mr. Hooper, take us over the limit. Sixty-one knots."

"Sixty-one knots, Comrade Captain."

Vazov swore under his breath and stared at the floor. Sixty knots was the maximum speed the *Charkov* had ever attained, although the chief engineer swore he could get another ten knots out of her. "Range?"

"About thirteen and a half kilometers, sir."

Still too far to risk firing a torpedo, Vazov realized, and ran his hand through his hair. Perhaps he should tell the helmsman to cut speed, even if the Americans got farther ahead.

"Captain!" Lieutenant Dragominov cried. "A power deviation in reactor number one. A four percent fluctuation. Already stabilizing."

"Damn!" Vazov fumed, wondering if the damage had just been done.

"A target!" Dave Jennings exclaimed. "Range is about eight and a half miles. Astern, almost due north."

Donovan felt as if an electric current pulsed through his body. He sat up, his eyes still glued to the viewscreen, and for an instant he saw it, the unmistakable dark contours of another ship, another sub represented by a solitary icon. Even as he focused on the icon, it disappeared.

"Contact is gone," Jennings announced.

Executive Officer Percy, who until that moment had demonstrated a marked skepticim, blurted, "I saw it, Captain."

"So did I," Donovan replied. "Now we know there *is* a sub stalking us, and they're slowly getting closer and closer. Since they haven't hailed us and are concealing their ship, we can only assume they have hostile intent and act accordingly."

"Should we try the sonar again at maximum power?"

"No. Whatever device they're using screens their sub from our sonar except for occasional echoes. And I don't want them to know we're on to them," Donovan said.

"If only they were within laser range," Percy mentioned.

"I know," Donovan stated, and looked at the helsman. "Mr. Hooper, reduce speed to one-half. Steady as she goes on our course to the Gilbert Islands."

Percy promptly came over to the chair. "Begging your pardon, sir, but is that wise?"

"Do you have an alternative?"

"Why not let them know we know they're there? We could try to jam their sonar. Or we could turn and head for their last known position, maybe force them into the open."

"Or maybe force them to fire a torpedo," Donovan countered. "No, we'll continue as is for the time being. Let them think they've fooled us. Buy ourselves some time."

"For what, sir?"

"To think, Mr. Percy. To think."

"And in the meantime they could launch a fish up our butt."

"They haven't fired yet, and they've been trailing us for days."

"So we just do nothing," Percy said glumly.

"There is one thing you can do."

"What's that, sir?"

"Sound alert stations."

"Comrade Captain, the American sub has cut speed to thirty knots and has resumed her bearing of one-seven-eight."

"So! We have fooled them, Comrades," Vazov said

169

happily. "They failed to detect us, and now they are once again en route to the Gilbert Islands, operating under the false assumption that all is well." He snorted. "Well, they shall learn their lesson the hard way."

"And now, Captain?" Dragominov asked.

"Now, Nikolai, we continue to stalk them. We will creep right up on them and tickle their ass, then fire our torpedoes up their rectum."

"Victory will be ours," the executive officer stated, although inwardly he lacked the conviction of his words. Inwardly, he wished they could open a channel and contact the American sub. Inwardly, he longed for the madness to end. But he dared not voice his beliefs under the current circumstances. Ivan Vazov might be his friend, but even Ivan had his limits where questioning duty was concerned.

"And once we have destroyed the imperialists, we will find an island, perhaps inhabited by friendly natives, and celebrate as we haven't celebrated in months," Vazov declared.

"My grandmother always told me to avoid putting the cart before the horse," Dragominov mentioned.

Vazov laughed. "My young friend, are you open to some constructive criticism?"

"Of course, Comrade Captain."

"You worry too much. You must learn to relax and enjoy life, to take what comes along in stride. You will live longer that way."

"Yes, Captain."

The roundtable discussion was actually held around Donovan's chair, with Executive Officer Percy, Systems Chief Smith, the first gunnery officer, and Alex Fisher in attendance. Communications Officer Jennings participated from his post at the communications console, and Helmsman Hooper lent an ear from the helm.

"I'm open to any and all suggestions," Donovan said to get the ball rolling. "Alex, you're our science officer. You read the article about the Domino 3000. If such a device is being used by the sub stalking us, what can we do about it? Does it have any weaknesses?"

"I wish I could tell you it does," Alex replied, "but I don't have the foggiest idea. The journal article I read was more a theoretical dissertation on the engineering aspects than a discussion of its strengths and weaknesses."

"What about the laser?" Percy queried. "If we could blast them with the laser, we might knock out their invisibility device."

"An excellent suggestion," Donovan said. "But for us to knock their device out, there are two prerequisites. First, they must get within range. As you well know, the laser's effective range in the weapon mode is only one thousand yards, maybe fifteen hundred at deeper levels. Second, we must know exactly where they're at or we'll miss."

"And so long as they're using this invisibility thing, we won't know exactly where they're at," Flaze interjected.

"Which is the crux of our problem," Donovan stressed. "If we could lock the laser on them in the probe mode, we might identify their screw signature. But, again, we must know their precise location."

"We're talking ourselves in circles," Charlie remarked. "We need to figure out a way to pinpoint their position. That's our first priority."

"Easier said than done," Donovan muttered, and happened to glance at the viewscreen. What he saw depicted there, rearing up from the ocean floor several miles ahead, made his pulse quicken. "Mr. Jennings, are they what I think they are?"

"Guyots, Captain."

Guyots. Submerged volcanic formations resembling enormous flat-topped mushroom stalks. Over seven hundred had been recorded in the Pacific, and many more were believed to be as yet undiscovered. Donovan stared at the holographic display, noting the proximity of the guyots to one another and the depth of their flat tops from the surface.

"Should we skirt them, Captain?" Jennings questioned.

"No," Donovan answered. "We're going straight through them."

"Straight through?" Percy repeated quizzically.

"Damn straight," Donovan said, and couldn't resist a smile. "Everyone to their posts."

"Where do you want me?" Charlie asked.

"And me?" chimed in Alex. I'll return to the sick bay if I'll be in the way."

"Stay where you are," Donovan told them. "I may need your advice."

Charlie leaned toward Alex. "It's hard to believe this is the same guy who would boot me out of his room when we were kids if I laid a hand on one of his precious toys," he whispered.

"Mr. Hooper," Donovan addressed the helmsman. "Steer us between those first two guyots. Try not to scrape the paint off the hull. Reduce speed to twenty knots."

"Aye, Captain. Reducing speed to twenty knots."

"Mr. Jennings, I need a computer projection and I need it yesterday. Feed the coordinates of the last two sonar contacts, that weak echo and the clear one, into the Cray-9. See if the computer can plot the target's speed and distance from *Liberator*."

The communications officer's eyes widened. "Yes,

sir. But that's a lot of information to extrapolate from such little data."

"I know, Mr. Jennings. Do your best."

"Are you planning an old-fashioned ambush, big brother?" Pirate inquired.

Donovan nodded. "If I can find the right spot."

"Mind filling me in?" Alex requested.

"Think of this as a game of hide-and-seek," Donovan replied. "Only instead of tagging a base, we're going to tag the fucker that's stalking us with a Mark 70 torpedo."

19

"Comrade Captain, the American sub is entering a guyot range."

Vazov pursed his lips, contemplating whether to follow the *Liberator* in among the guyots. Once, during war games conducted in the North Pacific, he had successfully eluded three Foxtrot-class diesel-electric submarines by hiding in a guyot range. The trio had been assigned to mimic American tactics during the exercise to give Vazov and the other Soviet commanders participating in the games simulated experience in fighting the imperialists.

Why was the *Liberator* entering the guyot range? Simply because the American captain saw no reason to deviate from his plotted course to the Gilberts? Or did the American know the *Charkov* stalked his ship? Was this a defensive stratagem of some sort? Vazov glanced at the sonar operator. "Range to the *Liberator?*"

"Slightly under thirteen kilometers, Captain."

"Their speed and our speed?"

"They are at twenty knots, Captain. We are at twenty-five."

Vazov nodded. The SHADOW system, automated in every other respect, could be adjusted by the operator to pursue enemy vessels at whatever speed was required. In an emergency the helmsman could override the automated system, but the override procedure frequently took longer than simply disengaging SHADOW. Soviet computers were still a shade slower than their American counterparts.

Vazov decided to stick to their current course and speed. He doubted the Americans were aware of the *Charkov*. The five-knot difference allowed the *Charkov* to slowly come up on the American sub from the rear, the most vulnerable area on any ship.

"Should we reduce speed, Captain?" Dragominov asked.

"No, Nikolai. If we were closer to their sub, I would. But at this range we will have ample warning if they try to trick us."

"We could bypass the guyots and resume stalking the Americans on the other side," the executive officer suggested.

"Too risky. I want them in front of us at all times. That way I know where they are."

Political Officer Vatutin approached them, all smiles. "Comrades. How much longer before we sink the Americans?"

"Several hours, at least," Vazov said.

"So long?"

"How many times must I tell you, Serge? Be patient. Stalking is a slow, slow process. The closer we get, the slower we'll go."

Vatutin frowned. "I know. I'm just impatient to get it over with."

"Impatience, Comrade Political Officer, is the deadliest of vices for a submarine commander to possess."

The sonar operator suddenly called out, "Captain, the target has increased speed to thirty knots."

Lines furrowed Vazov's brow as he turned toward

175

the SHADOW console. "Thirty knots? Then increase our speed to thirty-five."

Donovan's gaze was riveted to the viewscreen as his mind calculated probabilities. The first pair of guyots were one hundred feet astern, and five more were arranged in an uneven row directly ahead. Their flat tops were less than six hundred feet below the surface, higher than any he had ever seen. The holographic display also pictured three more of the strange mountains a half mile beyond the row, and one of the trio, the guyot in the middle, dwarfed all the others. "Mr. Hooper, when we're past this row increase speed to forty-five knots. Take us behind that big mother in the center of those other three."

"Yes, sir."

"Mr. Jennings, how is the computer projection coming along?"

"The Cray-9 is still working on it, Captain."

"Give it a swift kick."

Charlie moved to the left side of the chair. "What if the other skipper figures out your strategy?"

"Then our goose is cooked."

"I was hoping you wouldn't say that."

The communications officer was staring at the high-resolution monitor in front of him. "Here it is, Captain. The first contact was at a distance of nine miles. Target speed estimated at forty-five knots."

"What were we doing at the time?"

"Forty knots."

"I see. And the second contact?"

"Distance to the target about eight miles. Speed the same as ours. Sixty-one knots."

"So there's no pattern," Donovan said, and frowned.

"The Cray estimates the target to be seven and

a half to eight miles astern, depending on her speed."

"How soon will the other sub overtake us if we stop dead in the water?"

"Assuming the target is still moving at sixty-one knots, she'll overhaul us in seven to eight minutes. Assuming the other sub has slowed to forty-five knots, she'll catch us in ten to eleven minutes," Jennings said, then added, "But we have no way of knowing her current speed. She could be traveling at two knots for all we know."

"I doubt it," Donovan said. "And it's doubtful she'll come barreling up on us at forty-five knots. She seems to be going for a slow stalk. We forced her to increase speed earlier when we did, so we can discount the sixty-one-knot reading. Let's concentrate on the first contact. The target was doing five knots faster than we were. Let's assume she's still holding to that pattern. Let's figure she has been running five knots faster than us for some time and is still doing the same."

"That's not much to go on," Percy mentioned.

"It's all we *have,*" Donovan replied.

"Increasing speed to forty-five knots," Hooper interjected.

The gigantic guyot loomed larger and larger on the screen. Several hundred yards to the east and the west were the narrower formations.

"What's the width of the big one?" Donovan inquired.

"One thousand, four hundred fifty feet," Jennings answered.

More than enough, Donovan thought to himself. "Mr. Jennings, using the five-knot differential as the primary factor, have the Cray calculate how soon the other sub will catch up to us if we stop behind that huge guyot."

"Yes, sir."

Donovan sat on the edge of his seat, his hands gripping the arms of the chair. *Liberator* rapidly approached the enormous mountain, and watching the viewscreen he had the impression that the monolith was about to swallow the ship. "Mr. Hooper, take us around the west side of the guyot, then come about so the bow is pointing to the west. Hug the rear wall as close as you can."

"Understood, Captain. Taking us around the west side," Hooper said.

An undercurrent of tension had gripped everyone on the bridge. The red lights lent an austere aspect to each countenance, and the dozens of bright monitors cast a pale, ghostly luminescence on the faces of those sitting or standing nearby.

Donovan waited as Hooper skillfully skirted the guyot and brought *Liberator* about. "All stop!" he ordered. "Quiet ship."

"All stop!" Chief Smith repeated.

In moments *Liberator* coasted to a dead stop in the water, her bow to the west, her starboard side not more than fifty feet from the almost sheer rock wall.

"Laser to weapons status," Donovan directed.

"Weapons Control reports laser to weapons status," Jennings said.

"Mr. Percy, is the torpedo room ready?"

"Ready and willing, Captain."

"Good. Mr. Jennings, has the Cray provided those calculations yet?"

"Here they are, sir. The best the computer can do is narrow the time frame down to between sixteen and twenty minutes."

"It'll have to do," Donovan said.

"Captain, we have lost contact with the target."

"Slow to five knots," Vazov commanded, striding

178

over to the SHADOW operator. "SHADOW has lost its lock on the *Liberator?*"

"Yes, Comrade Captain. The cavitation sounds have ceased entirely."

Vazov did not like the news. No cavitation sounds meant the American sub must be drifting dead in the ocean, because every ship, no matter its size or type, produced the distinctive noise caused when a propellor churned the water. "Distance to the guyot range?"

"About twelve kilometers, Captain."

The executive officer materialized on Vazov's left. "Is it possible one of the guyots has come between them and us?"

"It is possible."

"But you don't sound convinced, Captain."

"I'm not," Vazov stated. He couldn't afford to commit a blunder now, and he decided he would rather err on the side of caution than waltz into a trap. If they did lose the *Liberator,* locating the American sub again should prove to be an easy task. They knew the course and destination of their enemies. What more could they ask for?

"Do you think the American commander is trying to trick us?"

"There is always that possibility, Nikolai," Vazov said.

"Will we go around the guyot range, then?"

"No, we will not," Vazov said. "SHADOW Operator, you will disengage all automated stalking systems."

"Disengaging, Captain."

"Helmsman Kuprevici, you will assume manual control of the ship."

"Control has been assumed, Comrade Captain."

"Build speed to twenty-five knots."

"Increasing speed, Captain."

"Sonar, you will be alert for any unusual sounds.

Anything—and I do mean *anything*—out of the ordinary must be reported immediately."

"Of course, Captain."

Vazov sensed rather than heard someone approach on his right, and he intuitively knew who it was before the political officer spoke.

"Has something gone wrong, Comrade?"

"We have temporarily lost contact with the *Liberator.*"

"How can such a thing happen? Our equipment is the best ever built."

"Our equipment is not infallible."

"Neither are our men."

Vazov glanced at Vatutin, a flinty gleam in his eyes. "Don't ever insult my crew again, Serge. I have trained many of them myself, and there are none better in the Soviet navy."

"We *are* the Soviet navy," Vatutin said irritably.

With the greatest of effort, Vazov resisted an impulse to smash the meddler in the mouth. Instead, he gazed at the navigator, then the sonar operator, wishing Vatutin would go play in one of the reactors. No such luck.

"You have disengaged SHADOW," the political officer noted.

Vazov said nothing.

"The Vostoy only functions when the SHADOW system is operational," Vatutin mentioned.

"The Vostoy is a component of the SHADOW system," Vazov corrected him.

"But now the Americans can pick us up on their sonar. Why would you switch off our veiling device and leave us vulnerable to an American attack?"

"Because, in a situation such as this, we are more vulnerable with the SHADOW system in operation."

"That is impossible."

Moron, Vazov thought. All political officers were

absolute morons. "When the SHADOW system is engaged, Comrade, the computer is running the ship. Even though we are invisible to enemy sonar, our reaction time to an enemy attack, should they somehow ascertain our position, is cut in half. The computer only shadows enemy vessels. It cannot fight a battle." He paused. "Which is why we are on manual. If the American commander has set a trap for us, we must be able to react instantly."

"But they will detect us for sure."

"Not if we are careful. Now, if you would be so kind, shut up. I have work to perform."

Vatutin's bulldog features turned a livid crimson, and for a few seconds he seemed about to throw himself at Vazov. Glaring wickedly, he wheeled and stalked from the control room.

Smirking, Vazov whispered to Dragominov, "There must be a God after all, eh?"

The executive officer's burst of laughter drew the attention of every seaman in the room.

"Comrades!" Vazov declared. "We have an American sub to find. Attend to your stations." His reprimand had the desired effect. To pound home his point he went from man to man, looking over their shoulders, knowing their diligence would increase a hundredfold.

The massive *Charkov* neared the guyot range on the same heading as *Liberator*. Hunched over at his post, his hands pressing the headphones tightly against his ears, the sonar operator listened to the echoes and watched the indicator on the panel.

Vazov watched his men perform with pride. The helmsman, Kuprevici, steered the submarine with consummate precision. In all his years at sea, Vazov had never seen anyone handle the helm better. The minutes dragged by as they covered the distance. "Distance to the range?" Vazov inquired after a while.

"Two thousand meters, Captain."

"How many guyots are there?"

"There are two dead ahead, then five in a row," the sonar operator disclosed, and adjusted a dial. "Wait. There are three more past those."

"And still no engine noises, no plant noises?"

"None, Captain."

Vazov moved to his helsman. "Ivachko, take us past the first pair of guyots."

"Between them or around them, Captain?"

"It doesn't matter."

"Then I will go around. You never know what could be hiding behind one of those mountains."

"No, you don't," Vazov agreed, and abruptly changed his mind. To follow the American sub into the heart of the guyot range would be a mistake. Better to play the part of the mouse than the cat. "When we are past the first pair, all stop," he ordered. "I think I know what the American commander is up to, and I know a way to turn the tables."

20

"Engine noises, Captain," Communications Officer Jennings stated, his voice level but an anxious edge to his tone.

Donovan scarcely breathed. This was more than he had dared hope for! His plan had been to wait in hiding behind the guyot, using the mountain to shield *Liberator* from the enemy's sonar, and direct all sensors to the west, acting on the belief that the other sub would follow *Liberator* through the guyots on the same general course. He had been relying on the ship's supersensitive detection equipment to pick up something, *anything*, that would allow them to get a laser lock on the stalking ship. The invisibility device might well screen the enemy sub from being detected head-on. But he wondered if any device could completely muffle the cavitation sounds, the noise made when the tiny bubbles created by the whirling propeller burst and drove the water back against the blades, and screen the sub from detection from the side or the rear. He had hoped to trick the enemy into drawing abreast of his position or even to pass *Liberator*. And here they were, coming toward him with their invisibility device off!

"Lots of noise, Captain. Bearing three-five-five. It's moving around the west side of the guyot. Distance difficult to determine because of the mountain. I'd say three hundred yards," Jennings reported, and paused. "Twin propellers."

"Then it isn't *Nemesis!* Can you get a screw signature match?"

The communications officer's whole body suddenly went rigid. "Affirmative, Captain. Positive screw signature identification. It's a Soviet Typhoon-class nuclear sub. Speed is only five knots."

For all of three seconds total astonishment reigned on the bridge. Crewmen exchanged astounded expressions. Many had suspected that a few Russian ships survived the war, but their conjectures did nothing to lessen the shock of actually encountering a Soviet vessel at such close proximity.

Executive Officer Percy snapped out of his daze first. "I knew it! I just knew some of those bastards made it through!"

Donovan stared at the holographic display, waiting for the Typhoon to materialize, and struggled to compose his surging emotions. After so many weeks, to finally make contact with the Russians took him a little by surprise. He'd presumed that the ship stalking them must be *Nemesis*. To find it was the enemy—

The *enemy?*

Donovan straightened, the thought giving him pause.

Did the Soviets believe World War Three was still in progress? They must. Why else had the Russian ship shadowed *Liberator* for days? But then, if the Soviets really did consider them adversaries, why hadn't the Typhoon attacked? The Soviets had had plenty of opportunity, what with their damn device rendering them virtually invisible.

Wait a minute. Donovan's eyes narrowed suspiciously. He was familiar with the Typhoon-class submarine, and none of them had carried invisibility apparatus. And, too, a Typhoon-class sub could never attain a speed in excess of sixty knots. Something was wrong here. As if to echo his sentiments, Jennings suddenly called out.

"Captain! We're picking up another noise."

"Can you identify it?"

"It sounds like another propeller, but it's so faint sonar can't get a fix on it."

Puzzled, aware that he had only a few more seconds in which to reach a decision, Donovan clenched his fists and barked, "As soon as we have a lock on the boomer, fire the laser in bursts. Rake her from bow to stern."

"The *laser?*" Percy repeated in disbelief.

"Aye, Captain," Jennings replied. "She'll clear the guyot in three, two, one! Now!"

Donovan's eyes widened in amazement as he saw the target appear on the Cyclops. Weapons Control automatically cut loose with the laser, and the hits were graphically shown on the screen as bright haloes of blue-green light. There was only one major problem.

"It's a torpedo!" Percy exclaimed.

Donovan came up out of the chair and took a half step, utterly confounded, watching the torpedo start to angle down toward the ocean floor.

"Direct hits," Jennings said. "All engine and prop noises have ceased."

Comprehension dawned, flooding Donovan's mind with insight and budding anxiety. The damn fish had been a decoy similar to the U.S. Navy's Remote Aiming Mobile Simulator, a mobile submarine simulator nicknamed RAMS. The decoy resembled a regulation torpedo, but its front half contained a high-power transducer linked to a tape recorder on which had been recorded the typical sounds made

185

by a Typhoon-class sub. Once fired, the simulator broadcasted the sounds to fool other craft. And I fell for it! Donovan thought.

"Captain, if that's not the Russian sub, where the hell is it?" Percy asked absently.

The words sent a chill rippling along Donovan's spine. "Damn! Mr. Hooper, hard left rudder!"

"Left full rudder," Hooper responded calmly, spinning the wheel to port, which in turn caused the bow to swing to the left, away from the guyot.

"All ahead full," Donovan commanded, still watching the dead decoy sink into the depths, its electronic circuitry disrupted by the laser blasts.

"All ahead full," Hooper repeated dutifully.

Donovan glanced at the communications officer. "Mr. Jennings, direct sonar astern at maximum power. Now!"

A few seconds earlier, the sonar operator aboard the *Charkov* had cocked his head while listening to the sounds in his headphones, a quizzical mien to his visage. "Something, Comrade Captain."

"What, Porfori?"

"I have never heard anything like it. A loud hissing. From behind the big guyot."

"We are losing contact with the decoy," the communications officer announced.

"Some new type of weapon?" Vazov speculated aloud, then looked at the helmsman. "Ivachko, take us around the east side of that guyot. Flank speed."

"Flank speed, Comrade Captain."

Vazov nodded in satisfaction. His plan had worked to perfection. After stopping and ensuring that the decoy was prepared for launching, he had ordered the *Charkov* forward at a speed of four knots. Slowly they had crept past the row of five guyots, and when he hadn't found the American sub hiding behind them, the obvious conclusion had

186

been that the *Liberator* was behind one of the last three mountains. And now he knew which one! "We have them, Nikolai!" he declared.

"It was almost too easy," Dragominov replied halfheartedly.

"Better them than us, my young friend."

The seconds seemed to stretch into eternity.

"Captain, we are coming around the guyot," Helmsman Kuprevici stated.

"Excellent. SHADOW Operator, engage the moment we're in the clear. Helmsman, override and assume manual control of steering and speed."

"Yes, Captain."

"Comrade Captain!" the sonar operator cried. "I am picking up propeller noises. It's the *Liberator.*"

"What did I tell you!" Vazov almost yelled, elated at his impending victory.

"Coming clear of the guyot, Captain," the SHADOW operator said. "Engaging SHADOW. Vostoy operational."

"Range?"

"Only seven hundred meters," the sonar operator said.

"Damn!" Vozov snapped, furious at being frustrated by the nearness to his foe. He couldn't fire a torpedo at such close range. Safety locks were installed on every torpedo to prevent them from detonating in their launch tube or close to the ship that fired them. In *Charkov*'s case, the torpedoes were set to arm at a distance of one thousand meters. If he fired a torpedo while the *Liberator* was under a thousand meters away, the shot would be a dud. "Damn!" he said again.

"Captain, target is fleeing. Speed is fifty-eight knots. Bearing is one-nine-zero. Range is now seven hundred and sixty meters."

"Prepare to fire," Vazov commanded. "Flood the tubes."

187

"Tubes are flooding, Captain."

"Open the outer torpedo doors."

A second elapsed before the response came back. "Outer torpedo doors are open."

"Good. As soon as the Americans are one thousand meters off, lock in the firing solution."

"Yes, Comrade Captain."

"We have a target astern," Communications Officer Jennings stated as an icon popped into view on the screen. Almost immediately the icon faded.

"They're using their invisibility device," Percy said.

"Were you able to get a target configuration?" Donovan inquired, his voice projecting an inner assurance. Now that the battle was joined, his years of training and experience served him in good stead, enabling him to maintain a composed, logical frame of mind.

"Yes and no, Captain," Jennings replied. "The target is not a Typhoon-class sub. Repeat. Not a Typhoon. Whatever she is, she's bigger and broader. The angle on her bow is nearly eighty degrees. That's all I could read before she faded out."

So the Soviets had constructed a new generation of submarines. Or was this one the only one in its class, like *Liberator?* Donovan placed his hands on his hips and scowled.

"She'll fire as soon as we're far enough away," Percy mentioned.

"I know," Donovan said, chiding himself for his stupidity. He should have known! When the other sub had failed to show up after twenty minutes, he should have known they were about to pull a fast one. This is what a lack of combat experience does, he thought, and resolved to do better. "Mr. Hooper, change course to two-seven-zero."

"Changing course, Captain."

"Prepare for jamming."

"Comrade Captain, the American sub is changing course."

"New heading?"

"Two-seven-zero."

"Adjust the firing solution accordingly. Range?"

"Nine hundred meters and climbing."

"In exactly one hundred meters, fire one and two."

"Any second now," Percy said.

Donovan's gaze was riveted to the screen. He spied them an instant after sonar registered their presence.

"Two fish astern," Jennings announced cooly. "The Russians have fired two torpedoes. Distance is one thousand, ninety-three yards. Speed, fifty-nine knots. Climbing rapidly."

"Jam them," Donovan directed.

"Attempting jamming," Jennings responded, wondering if there would be time. He already had the acoustical jamming apparatus fired up, but the fish were so close. So damn close. Don't think about that! he thought. Think about timing the jamming pulses to match the sonar impulses from the torpedoes. Think about getting the pulse repetition rate right. Think about the ghost targets the jamming would create, targets that would confuse the torpedoes. Targets that might make the fish miss. Might.

Donovan wasn't about to rely strictly on the jamming to save their hides. Evasive action was called for. "Mr. Hooper, are we at flank speed?"

"Sixty-one knots, Captain."

"When I give the word, lean on the rudder."

"Aye, Captain."

"Mr. Percy, all hands brace for possible impact."

"Yes, sir," Percy said, and flashed the appropriate message throughout the ship.

"Jamming is under way," Jennings said. "Fish are now at sixty-nine knots. Range is eight hundred yards."

The torpedoes were displayed on Cyclops as twin spears lancing toward *Liberator,* their small engines churning the water behind them.

"Screw signatures identify the torpedoes as Tigerfish," Jennings reported mechanically, still concentrating on the jamming. Tigerfish were the best torpedoes the Soviet navy possessed, and they were deucedly difficult to deceive. The jamming pulses continued to bombard them. Come on! Take the bait!

"Comrade Captain, the Americans are trying to jam our torpedoes."

"To be expected. Let them try. Are the torpedoes still on course?"

"There has been no deviation, Captain. The sonar lock is constant."

"Then the imperialists are finished."

"Yes, Captain."

Vazov pondered for a moment. "But just to be on the safe side, lock in the firing solution for three and four."

"Locking in."

"And prepare five and six for firing."

"Four hundred yards," Jennings disclosed.

"Speed?"

"Sixty-nine knots and still climbing."

Donovan's lips compressed in a thin line. It wouldn't be long now. The torpedoes on the viewscreen were growing larger with each second. Now they resembled squat, streaking javelins, metallic lances programmed to puncture *Liberator*'s hull.

"Three hundred yards," Jennings said.

"Come on! Jam those fuckers!" Percy declared passionately, a rare display for him.

"Two hundred yards."

Donovan sat down and grasped the arms of his chair. His skin was tingling and his lungs seemed to be on vacation. He couldn't have torn his eyes from the screen if he tried.

"One hundred yards."

"The jamming hasn't worked!" Charlie exclaimed. "They're going to hit."

21

"Don't count us out yet," Donovan said.

Except for Communications Officer Jennings and Helmsman Hooper, all eyes were on the Cyclops display. They saw the Tigerfish bearing straight and true. Then, at eighty yards, the torpedo on the left abruptly slanted down, going for the bottom. But the right-hand fish continued racing at *Liberator*, exceeding her speed, unerringly on target.

Beads of sweat coated Dave Jennings's forehead as he concentrated on fine-tuning the jamming signals, his hands working the dials feverishly, absently gnawing on his lower lip in his nervousness. Turn, damn you! Turn! his mind shrieked.

Seventy yards and closing.

A stubborn son of a bitch, aren't you? Jennings thought, continuing to fine-tune. Some torpedoes were guided to their targets by internal computer homing systems, while others were directed by the launching vessel through the means of an insulated cable that ran between the vessel and the fish. The Tigerfish were state-of-the-art. They possessed sophisticated internal homing systems, and they were extremely difficult to deceive.

Sixty yards and still closing.

Jennings resisted the temptation to look at the viewscreen. He had to concentrate, concentrate,

concentrate. If only the fish would go for one of the ghost targets he had created. There were several to choose from. Pick one, damn you!

Fifty yards, and the Tigerfish began to veer to the right. The deviation was slight, and for a breathtaking moment it appeared the torpedo would strike the sub. On the holographic display the fish seemed to miss the hull by mere inches, then sped off into the depths.

"Hard left rudder, Mr. Hooper," Donovan stated. "Get us the hell out of here."

"Hard left rudder, sir."

"New course will be one-seven-zero at flank speed."

"One-seven-zero at flank speed."

"Mr. Jennings."

"Yes, Captain?"

"That was a job well done."

"Thank you, Captain. It got a bit hairy there for a while," the communications officer replied.

"It may get hairy again."

"Comrade Captain, the Americans jammed both of our torpedoes," said the sonar operator.

"Damn them!"

"They are on a new bearing of one-seven-zero. Speed is about sixty knots."

"They won't escape our wrath so easily. Do we have a firing solution for three and four?"

"Yes, Comrade Captain."

"Then fire three and four."

"More fish in the water," Dave Jennings said loud and clear. "Range is two thousand yards. Speed is fifty-one knots and increasing."

"Not this time," Donovan said under his breath, then glanced at his executive officer. "Mr. Percy, if they can play games with decoys, then so can we."

"Preparing decoy for launch, Captain."

Donovan nodded. The RAMS would emit the same sounds as *Liberator,* only louder, and hopefully lure the Tigerfish toward it and not the sub. Communications would steer the decoy away from *Liberator* where the torpedoes could detonate harmlessly.

"Nineteen hundred yards and sixty-two knots," Jennings said.

"Any sign of the Russian sub?"

"None, sir."

"Did you get a fix on the point where she fired her fish?"

"Yes, Captain. She fired the first pair from near the east side of the guyot. The second pair were fired from two hundred yards farther east."

"So the Russian skipper isn't staying in one place. Smart. Real smart."

"May I ask a question?" Alex unexpectedly inquired. She had been standing stock-still, her hands gripping the back of the captain's chair, her features ashen, alternately fascinated and frightened by the activity swirling around her. Back in San Francisco, where she had fought the dreaded whiteshirts with distinction, the battleground had been familiar. The enemy, however horrible, had been living beings composed of flesh and blood. But this was so different. So alien. The enemy could dispense death from hundreds and thousands of yards away. She had no control over the situation. She couldn't fight back. And her helplessness, more than the actual combat, filled her with dread.

"In a second," Donovan answered, engrossed in the screen.

"The decoy is ready, Captain," Percy said.

"Outer door open?"

"Yes, sir."

"Then launch the RAMS."

"The decoy is away, sir."

"Mr. Jennings, swing the decoy back toward the fish."

"Turning the RAMS, Captain."

The Remote Aiming Mobile Simulator appeared on the Cyclops display, speeding in a tight loop, heading for the approaching Tigerfish. The latest in a long line of decoys, the RAMS could be guided with hair's-breadth precision to any point desired, unlike its predecessors, which had to be programmed for a specific course prior to launch.

"Activate the transducer."

"Activating." At the flick of a switch, Jennings sent the simulated sounds of *Liberator* blasting at the torpedoes.

"They have launched a decoy, Comrade Captain, and are trying to draw our torpedoes off target."

Vazov swore. "Are the Tigerfish still locked on the sub?"

"So far, yes."

"Helmsman Kuprevici, you will hold our position in case I decide to fire five and six."

"Holding, Captain."

"Porfori, have the torpedoes deviated yet?"

"Still on course, sir."

"We could teach the Americans a thing or two about building reliable decoys, eh?"

"Distance between the RAMS and the Tigerfish is now one thousand yards," Jennings reported.

"Let's find out if the fish are locked on us or the decoy," Donovan said. "Steer the RAMS to the east on a bearing of zero-four-five."

"New bearing is zero-four-five."

Alex heard Executive Officer Percy laugh. What on earth could the man find so funny at a time like this? she wondered.

195

* * *

Sonar Operator Porfori did a double take, staring at his indicator, then double-checked his headphones. "Captain, the American decoy has changed course. New heading is zero-four-five."

"Zero-four-five?" Vazov repeated, mentally envisioning the position of both submarines, the torpedoes, and the damn decoy. Suddenly he stiffened. "And the Tigerfish?"

Porfori was a study in intensity. He listened for several seconds, then blanched. "The torpedoes are homing on the decoy. They have lost their lock on the American sub."

"Son of a bitch! Has the heading changed?"

"No, Comrade Captain."

Hissing, Vazov spun. "Helmsman Kuprevici, left full rudder! All ahead full!"

Executive Officer Dragominov, standing a meter behind his mentor, was puzzled by the sudden panic in his superior officer's tone until he performed a few computations of his own. Despite their predicament, he felt a measure of admiration for the American commander.

"The bastard!" Vazov railed. "He is sending the Tigerfish back in our general direction, hoping they will hit us!"

"You said he was cagey."

"Yes, but he is too cagey for our good," Vazov responded angrily. "Porfori, what is the range between the torpedoes and us?"

"Nine hundred and twenty meters."

"And between the torpedoes and the decoy?"

"Four hundred and ten meters, Captain. The decoy is still on a heading of zero-four-five, and the Tigerfish have almost completed their swing."

"Where is the *Liberator?*"

"On a course of one-seven-zero. Speed, sixty

knots. Distance is two thousand, seven hundred meters."

"They are using the decoy to cover their escape," Vazov said, and shook his head. "I will never make the mistake of underestimating the American commander again."

"Distance to the torpedoes is nine hundred meters," the sonar operator said. "The torpedoes are closing on the decoy. Three hundred and ninety meters to go."

"Good. We will have a five- or six-hundred-meter safety margin," Vazov said. "More than enough."

"But it will get a bit bumpy," Dragominov noted.

"So?" Vazov smiled. "A good case of the shakes will make the men work that much harder."

Dragonimov scanned the control room. "What happened to Comrade Vatutin? I'm surprised he has not returned by now."

A derisive snort came from Vazov. "He is probably hiding under his bunk, quaking in fear. The man only knows how to fight with his mouth."

"The men might hear you, Comrade."

"Who cares? I am tired of treating that pompous ass with special consideration. He is a liability to our crew and we must deal with him sooner or later."

"What do you mean by deal with him?"

Before Vazov could respond, the sonar operator called out, "One hundred meters between the decoy and our torpedoes."

"Brace for shock waves," Vazov ordered.

The command was given. Everyone focused on the sonar operator.

"Fifty meters," Porfori said. "Forty."

"This will work to our advantage, Nikolai," Vazov commented. "You'll see."

"Thirty meters."

"How, Comrade Captain?"

197

"Twenty meters."

"Because now the American commander will have no idea where we are at. We can take him completely by surprise and come at him from any direction."

"Ten meters. Nine."

"Yes," Vazov went on. "We can still finish the *Liberator* off before the day is over."

"Five-four-three-two-one."

They all heard the explosion, even through the hull, a muffled detonation that signified the torpedoes had finally caught up with the decoy. In seconds the shock waves struck the *Charkov,* and despite the attack submarine's immense size the waves rolled the ship from side to side. Vazov, Dragominov, and the other officers snatched at nearby stanchions, consoles, or railings to prevent themselves from falling flat.

Dragominov was reminded of the time his father had taken him out in a rowboat and the pair had been caught in a surprise spring storm. The lake had been transformed from a placid reservoir into a raging maelstrom in minutes. Nikolai's father had rowed frantically toward shore, but his powerful strokes could make scant progress against the unbridled fury of Nature unleashed. The waves had tossed their small rowboat as if it were constructed of paper instead of wood. Dragominov had held on for his life, terrified to his core, and watched the waves slap the rowboat about, a plaything in the grip of elemental forces. And now he felt a similar sensation.

Vazov, oddly, smiled. To him this was part and parcel of a sub commander's job, the part he liked the most. He had always enjoyed war games, always looked forward to the time he could actually engage an enemy in combat. His wish had finally been granted, and the battle was made all the sweeter by the knowledge that he was avenging the deaths of his loved ones. Ludmila, Iosif, and Vsevolod would smile in their graves when they saw him in his hour of shining glory.

The buffeting gradually subsided and the *Charkov* settled in the water, still on an easterly course.

"Damage report!" Vazov barked.

"No structural damage reported, Captain. All systems are functional."

"Then we shall bring this chase to its inevitable conclusion. Ivachko, the Americans fled to the south. We shall pursue them. One-eight-zero at flank speed."

"One-eight-zero at flank speed."

"Do you really think the Americans are running from us?" Dragominov asked.

"Is there any doubt?" Vazov responded. "They know they do not stand a chance against our superior technology. How can they fight what their sonar can't see?" He paused, smirking. "I never realized how invincible we are with the Vostoy in operation. No one can defeat us."

"Excuse me for saying this, Comrade, but such overconfidence can be dangerous."

"Overconfidence?" Vazov repeated, and snickered. "Did the imperialists fire a torpedo at us? No. Did they even attempt to engage us? No. They knew better. To them we are invisible, and our invisibility makes us unbeatable."

"I recall reading a book when I was a child," Dragominov mentioned. "It wasn't on the approved list, but it wasn't banned, either. It was written long ago by an Englishman named Wells, and the story concerned an invisible man who thought he was invincible, too."

"What happened to him?"

"He was killed by a mob."

"Are you implying there is a lesson to be learned from the story?"

"Perhaps, Comrade Captain."

Vazov frowned. "Sometimes, my young friend, you worry me. The *Liberator* will be on the bottom by nightfall. Mark my words."

What on earth had all that swaying and shaking been about?

Political Officer Serge Vatutin slowly straightened in his chair and released his hold on the small gray table that had been positioned in the center of his cabin when the shaking began, and that now was pressed up against his bunk. He wondered if the ship had been hit, and fear seized him at the thought of being drowned. If he were to have his choice of deaths, drowning would be at the very bottom of the list. He listened, but there was no alarm. So whatever had caused the swaying had not been serious.

Relieved, he stared at the vodka bottle in his left hand, the bottle he normally kept stashed at the bottom of his footlocker. But not now, not when he had been handed the ultimate insult. Not when drinking was the only thing that soothed his troubled mind anymore.

Vatutin glanced at the doorway, debating whether to venture to the control room to find out what was going on. The table and his chair had both nearly upended, and he was amazed they were still upright. He took another swig of vodka.

The pompous ass, he thought.

All submarine commanders were pompous asses,

201

and he should know, because he had served under three of the bastards during his illustrious career.

They all believed they were so high and mighty!

Vatutin snorted and took another gulp, ignoring the trickle that ran from the left corner of his mouth, over his chin, and down his neck. His brown eyes focused, with an effort, on the small case containing his commendations, which he had attached to the aft bulkhead, and his visage hardened. He had devoted his life to the Motherland and been rewarded several times for his competence and loyalty. So why, then, did assholes like Ivan Vazov seem to be intent on belittling him at every opportunity? Why had every sub commander he'd known treated him with ill-concealed contempt?

The sons of bitches!

Sub commanders were always so damn smug, always so certain they were right about everything.

Vatutin hated them. All of them. He swallowed more vodka and stared at the other walls of his cabin, one of the largest on the ship, then at the photograph of V. I. Lenin hanging above his bunk. There was a man he would have liked to work with, a man who understood the psychology of the masses, who knew what it was like to be a dedicated Communist in a world where dedication to any ideal was a rare commodity.

A man who would not have tolerated Vazov's insolence!

Vatutin knew the sub commander disliked him. He could tell by the condescending tone the captain used when addressing him. He could tell by the occasional flickers of scorn discernible in the other's eyes. He could tell by the way Vazov's mouth curled perceptibly downward whenever he approached.

And now the bastard had told him to shut up in front of the men!

Rage rose within Vatutin like a tidal wave, and

he pounded his right fist on the table again and again, venting his resentment, but even that failed to quell his turbulent emotions. Incensed beyond endurance, he stood unsteadily, his equilibrium affected by the half bottle of vodka he had imbibed, and proceeded to hurl the table against the bulkhead. Still infuriated, he picked up his chair and slammed it against the bulkhead, too, not once but three times. Only then did he regain control, and with an oath he tossed the chair aside.

Do you see, Vazov? he wanted to shout.

Do you see what you have made me do?

"Sounds, Comrade Captain."

Vazov stepped over to the sonar operator. "What do you mean by sounds, Porfori?"

"Pounding, Captain."

"At what distance? Give me a bearing."

Porfori looked up, his face expressing complete bafflement. "The pounding, Captain, is coming from inside the *Charkov.*"

"What?"

"Bingo," Communications Officer Jennings said. "We have them, Captain. We're picking up loud knocking noises."

"Knocking noises?"

"That's the only way I can describe them. They're not engine noises. It's like someone is beating on a hull with a hammer. Bearing is zero-nine-zero. Range is three thousand yards. Speed, sixty knots."

"Can we get a laser lock on the target?"

"Negative, Captain. The noises have already ceased."

"At least we have a good idea where they are," Donovan said. "Good job, Mr. Jennings. Keep monitoring on passive only."

"Yes, sir."

Donovan congratulated himself on his successful ruse. He had taken *Liberator* to the south at flank speed for two miles, then turned to the west for a mile and stopped her dead in the water. He had no intention of staying on the defensive any longer. So far, the Russians had called all the shots. All that was about to change.

"Can I ask my question now?" Alex inquired.

"Just a minute," Donovan responded. "Mr. Hooper, let's see if we can give the Soviets a taste of their own medicine. Our heading will be one-three-five at forty knots."

"One-three-five at forty knots, sir."

Donovan shifted in his chair and smiled at Alex. "So what's your question?"

She surveyed the equipment on the bridge, the consoles, computers, and monitors, and sighed. "You have to understand that I'm relatively new at this war business. There's a lot I don't know."

"You're not alone. I've taken part in countless practice exercises and fared well at war games, but there's no substitute for actual experience. This is my first war, too."

Alex nodded. "But you were trained for this. You know what to expect. I don't, and I'm a little confused."

"About what?"

"The laser, for instance. You employed the laser to stop that decoy, but you didn't use the laser against the four torpedoes. Why not?"

"The idea never occurred to me," Donovan admitted. "The designers of our weapons systems never intended for the laser to be used against torpedoes, for several reasons. First, torpedoes travel too fast and they're too small to ensure an accurate hit. I know we took out the decoy, but it was only moving at five knots at close range and we had

204

plenty of time to set up the laser lock in advance. The laser is meant to be used against other ships."

"What are the other reasons?"

"Second, the laser only *disrupts* circuits and the results are often unpredictable. We can't predict exactly which circuits the laser will play havoc with, and when we're dealing with a live torpedo we can't afford to take chances. Remember *Nemesis?* We hit her with the laser, but that didn't stop her from escaping under full power."

"What else?"

"There's a remote chance the laser could cause a torpedo to detonate, and some of those fish carry a warhead packed with enough explosive to tear a battleship in half. *Liberator* is rated to survive a near hit, but I don't want to put our hull to the test if I don't have to."

"Okay. Now I understand. But what would you say if I told you I might be able to develop a computer program that would enable you to use the laser against torpedoes consistently with predictable results?"

"I'd say develop the program. Flaze and Hooper can help you. They know more about *Liberator*'s systems than anyone else."

"I'll get on it first chance I have."

Donovan smiled and glanced at his brother. "How are you holding up, Pirate?"

"Just fine. I've learned a very valuable lesson today."

"Oh?"

"I'll never make a career out of the Navy," Charlie quipped.

"Sub combat can be somewhat harrowing."

"Somewhat? My hair turned gray, or didn't you notice?"

"Hang in there," Donovan said. He faced forward. "Mr. Jennings, anything more on the Soviet sub?"

"No, Captain."

"Keep at it. We're bound to pick up something sooner or later. Cavitation sounds. Their sonar, maybe. They made a major mistake in letting us get behind them. It'll cost them."

"Here we go again," Charlie said.

"We *lost* them? How can we have lost them?" Vazov demanded angrily.

"They must be beyond our sonar range, Captain."

"Impossible, Porfori. They did not have that much of a head start."

"I hear nothing, Captain."

Exasperated, Vozov turned toward the SHADOW operator. "Are we still on the same heading the Americans were taking?"

"Yes, Captain."

"Then they must be somewhere in front of us. All stop! Sonar, you will conduct a search forward on all active systems."

"Conducting a search, Captain."

Dragominov stepped forward. "Comrade, the Americans might be able to fix our position." Sonar pulses, he knew, could work both ways. The Americans were bound to hear the pinging and locate the source.

"By the time they do, Nikolai, we will be somewhere else."

A frown curved Dragonimov's mouth. His mentor was being uncharacteristically careless and the negligence could well cost all of them their lives. Was Ivan so intent on avenging his family that he would even sacrifice the *Charkov?* No, Dragominov decided. His superior officer was too much the professional to permit personal feelings to interfere with his job performance.

He hoped.

"Captain, the Soviets are trying to get a bearing on us. They're on active sonar and they're pinging the hell out of the water south of their position."

"Which is?"

"About two miles southeast of us. They've stopped, Captain. Depth is one thousand feet, the same as ours."

"Helmsman Hooper, increase our speed to sixty knots. If they're so busy scaring the fish, they might not notice us until it's too late."

Hooper beamed. "Increasing speed to sixty knots."

"As soon as we're within range, I want a laser lock on that sub. Tell Weapons Control to fire the second they have the lock. Don't wait for an order from me."

"Aye, Captain."

"Mr. Percy, are one and two ready for firing?"

"They've *been* ready, Captain."

"Then stand by. You're about to have that revenge you've wanted."

"Yes, *sir!*"

"Still nothing?"

"Nothing, Comrade Captain. No noises whatsoever," Porfori reported.

Vazov clasped his hands behind his back and began to pace. The *Liberator* had fled south at sixty knots, and he had started in pursuit at the same speed immediately after eluding the Tigerfish. So the Americans could not have had more than a three- or four-minute head start. Five at the very most. Which meant they *must* be close to the *Char-*

kov. They must be within four or five kilometers to the south.

A thought made him halt abruptly.

What if he had miscalculated? What if the American commander had decided to fight instead of fleeing? What if the *Charkov* had already passed the American sub? He licked his suddenly dry lips and wheeled.

"Helmsman Kuprevici, right full rudder."

"Right full rudder, Captain."

"Sonar, continue to search for the American sub."

"No noises yet, Captain."

Dragominov noted the worried expression on his superior officer and came closer. "Is anything wrong, Comrade?"

"Perhaps you were right after all, my young friend. Perhaps it is better to be a worrier."

"Do you think they are behind us?"

"I don't know. I hope to God they are not."

"God, Comrade?"

Communications Officer Jennings listened intently for a moment. "Captain, their active sonar is shifting from south to west. They might be executing a turn."

"Damn," Donovan said softly. "Distance to the target?"

"Now approximately one mile."

Too far to use the laser! Donovan gazed at the Cyclops display, wishing he could see the enemy depicted there. He didn't quite realize how dependent he had become on the holographic representation until then. How easily we adapt, he thought, and looked at Percy.

Jennings spoke up again. "They're definitely turning, Captain."

Donovan had a choice to make. Either fire a torpedo, which would only have the sound waves from the Soviet sonar to guide it and might well miss, or try to get close enough to fire the laser in the hope that the invisibility device would be disrupted and the Russian ship would finally become visible. If he didn't fire the torpedo, he ran the risk of losing the Soviet sub again.

Apparently thinking the same thing, Percy said, "We won't get within laser range before they come about. We should fire a torpedo now while we have the chance."

"Hold your fire, Mr. Percy. You'll get your chance," Donovan said, deciding to try for the laser shot first. Rendering the Soviet sub visible was more important than possibly scoring with a Mark 70. If he was wrong, if the Soviets completed their turn before *Liberator* came within laser range, then he would have to bear the responsibility and the blame if the Russians scored first.

"Captain!" Dave Jennings declared. "The Soviet sub has swung toward us!"

23

"How dare you, Ivan Vazov!"

Every seaman and officer in the control room turned toward the speaker, and every man was shocked to behold the political officer framed in the aft doorway, an empty bottle of vodka dangling from his left hand, his features livid. Even the sonar operator glanced around, neglecting his screen, dumfounded by the intrusion.

"Comrade Vatutin!" Vazov stated sternly. "What is the meaning of this?"

"I demand an apology," Vatutin growled, slurring his words, and shuffled forward.

"An apology?"

"For humiliating me in front of the crew. I demand a public apology, *Comrade*," Vatutin said, accenting the last word scornfully.

"Now is not the time for this," Vazov said. "Return to your cabin and sober up."

"Do you think I am drunk?"

"I *know* you are drunk," Vazov replied, and turned to the sonar operator. "Anything yet?"

Porfori studied his indicators and listened. Suddenly he tensed and blanched. "Contact, Captain! Bearing is two-nine-zero. Range—fourteen hundred meters!"

"Fourteen hundred!" Vazov repeated, stunned.

He recovered instantly and barked orders. "Go to passive so they cannot get a lock on us! Helmsman, right full rudder. Ahead all full!"

"Right full rudder," Kuprevici responded.

Not a meter away, Executive Officer Dragominov reached for a nearby stanchion and gripped it tightly. He kept repeating the distance over and over in his mind. Fourteen hundred meters. Fourteen hundred meters. And the Americans must have a fix on the *Charkov*'s position, thanks to the damn sonar! We are done for, he thought, and braced for a torpedo.

"We have laser lock. Weapons Control is commencing fire!"

Donovan sat on the edge of his chair, riveted to the screen, watching the bursts of blue-green light flash from *Liberator* and appear to strike empty ocean. The bursts danced and sparkled, a miniature underwater aurora borealis, a spectacular display the equal of any July Fourth celebration, dazzling in its brilliance.

"Direct hit, Captain!"

Captain First Rank Ivan Vazov scanned his control room, aghast at the crackling sounds he heard and the puffs of white and black smoke coming from several equipment banks. "What is happening?" he bellowed. *"Someone tell me what is happening!"*

"We are losing the Vostoy," the SHADOW operator cried. A cloud of smoke had billowed from the SHADOW console, enshrouding his head. He coughed and frantically manipulated the controls.

"Compensate! Keep the Vostoy operational!" Vazov thundered. "The Americans will see us if the Vostoy goes down."

The SHADOW operator, swatting the smoke

aside with his left hand, looked at his commander. "The Vostoy *is* down, Comrade Captain."

Dragominov heard and swallowed hard.

"There she is!" Percy exclaimed.

One moment the Cyclops display had shown only the expanse of water below, the surface above, and the glittery light show. The next, the Soviet sub blinked into view, materializing as if from thin air, her every feature depicted in stark detail.

"She's running, Captain," Jennings announced.

"Slow to forty knots," Donovan commanded.

"Slowing to forty knots," Hooper replied.

"Mr. Percy, fire one!"

"One away!"

A Mark 70 long-range, acoustic-homing torpedo leaped from the bow of *Liberator* and sped toward the Soviet ship, rapidly attaining its top speed of seventy knots, unerringly on target.

"Contact in twelve point eight seconds."

"All stop! Brace for shock waves!"

Charkov was doing sixty knots, bearing to the south-southeast, when the Mark 70 struck her on the port side, just aft of the control room. The five-hundred-pound warhead in the torpedo's blunt nose detonated on impact, and the resultant explosion tore a fifteen-foot-wide hole in the sub's outer hull and crumpled the adjoining sections, her hull plates buckling as if crushed in the fist of an invisible giant.

Fifteen feet separated *Charkov*'s outer hull from her inner, and despite the presence of one of the sub's water-filled ballast tanks between the hulls at the point of impact, the blast created a series of cracks in the pressure hull. Water began to pour into the submarine, shooting from the cracks with all the pressure of a fire hose. One of the cracks developed in a bulkhead in the control room, another in the casing of reactor number one.

Nikolai Dragominov held on to the stanchion, his shoulders straining, as the sub rocked and bounced. He saw Captain Vazov fly through the air and smash into a console, and he grimaced as his mentor rolled over. Vazov's eyes were closed and blood was pouring from a jagged gash in the center of his forehead. Other seamen were crashing against bulkheads or tumbling over one another as the explosion buffeted the vessel. The bow abruptly tilted downward at a thirty-degree angle.

"Help me, Comrade!"

Dragominov turned in the direction of the petrified voice in time to see Political Officer Vatutin slam into an instrument panel and collapse on the deck underneath one of the spurting cracks, his nostrils crushed, his lips crushed to a pulp.

Many of the seamen were screaming.

"A direct hit, Captain," Communications Officer Jennings announced. "Her engines have stopped. There are all sorts of hull-popping noises. I think her pressure hull has been breached." He listened for several seconds, his countenance sobering. "I think she's starting to sink."

"All right!" Percy declared happily.

Donovan simply watched the viewscreen, noting the sub's lopsided slant, and wondered if the control room had been vented to the sea. Oddly enough, he did not feel particularly elated at his victory. He thought of the dozens of Soviet seamen who must be dying at that very moment, and the realization precluded any inclination to gloat.

"Ready with number two," Percy said.

"Stand by."

"But we can finish the bastards off, Captain."

"They already are finished."

* * *

Dragominov released the stanchion and waded through ankle-deep water to Ivan Vazov. He knelt and cradled Vazov's head in his lap, and only then did he see how deep the gash truly was, a terrible wound that had split the cranium and exposed the brain. Blood and a pale fluid seeped out onto his shirt. Mechanically, he felt for a pulse. There was none. He felt an urge to weep.

"Comrade, what do we do?"

The frantic words and strong hands on his shoulder drew Dragominov out of himself, and he twisted to discover Helmsman Kuprevici at his side.

"What do we do?" Kuprevici repeated in desperation.

"We get a grip on ourselves and perform as seamen," Dragominov said. He gently deposited his mentor on the deck, then stood. The acrid smoke tingled his nose. Water continued to spray into the control room. Bodies were scattered here and there. Sailors were helping their comrades to stand or tending injuries. He took a deep breath and spoke calmly but forcefully. "Comrades! There is not a second to lose! We must restore our buoyancy and head for the surface with all deliberate speed. Our injured must wait. All hands to their stations! Move!"

They responded to his orders swiftly, almost eagerly, reacting as much to his promise of salvation as his authoritative tone.

"Communications, open a channel to the American sub."

"Comrade?"

"Do it!"

"I will try."

Dragominov surveyed the control room, making an estimate of which systems appeared to be intact and which obviously were out of commission. "I

214

need a damage control report right away. We must get the pumps working. We must stabilize our trim. All of you know your duty. Move, Comrades, move!"

"Engineering reports reactor number one has been damaged and reactor number two has been shut down. We are on battery power."

Dragominov nodded. "We will get out of this alive if we keep our wits about us."

"Captain, it's them."

"Who?" Donovan responded, and forever after, whenever he recalled the incident, he would experience a twinge of dismay over having asked such a ridiculous question.

"The Russians, sir. They want to talk."

"Don't trust them, Captain," Percy stated. "It could be a trick."

"Pipe them through the speaker," Donovan instructed. "Let everyone hear this."

Jennings flicked a few switches. "Whenever you're ready, sir."

"This is Captain Thomas Donovan of the U.S.S. *Liberator*. To whom am I speaking?"

"This is Executive Officer Nikolai Dragominov aboard the *Charkov*. We have ceased all hostilities. Our ship has been severely damaged and we request your assistance."

"Why should I trust you?"

"Please, Captain. I do not have time to bandy words. Our ship is slowly flooding." There came a pause. "Our commanding officer has been killed and I am in charge. I want this madness to *end.*"

The sincerity conveyed, even over the tinny speaker, stirred Donovan's admiration. "What can we do to help you?"

"We are going to try and make it to the surface. If you would be so kind, could you follow us up? We

215

require medical assistance. Our doctor was killed in the explosion."

Donovan barely hesitated. "We will follow you to the surface and render whatever assistance we can. I, too, would like to see this madness end."

"Thank you, Captain. With all my heart, thank you. Over."

Static crackled from the speaker as the link was severed.

"Well, what do you know," Donovan said to no one in particular, and leaned back in his swivel chair. "Mr. Percy, we will do as the Russian requests and follow them to the surface."

"We could be making a mistake, Captain."

"At the first sign of treachery we'll sink them. Satisfied?"

"Yes, sir."

A soft sigh fluttered from Donovan's lips, and he rested his chin in his right hand. "Mr. Jennings, what are the Soviets doing now?"

"They have their ship on an even keel. There are no reactor plant noises so they must be on battery power."

"Range?"

"About twelve hundred yards."

"Mr. Hooper, you will close to within a thousand yards of their stern. Easy does it. Say twenty knots."

"Twenty knots. Aye, Captain."

Alex came around the right side of the chair and regarded Donovan quizzically.

"What's with you?"

"It's nice to know you're not as bloodthirsty as I thought you were."

"Where did you ever get an idea like that?"

"Oh, when you nuked the white-shirts in San Francisco. Right then and there I knew you were not to be trifled with."

216

"Thanks. I think."

"What will you do with the Russians?"

"To be honest, I haven't thought that far ahead. We can escort them to the nearest landfall, which would be the Gilbert Islands, provided their ship holds up. After that, I don't really know. A lot depends on their attitude. If they're friendly, we can help them establish a base of their own, or we might even ask them to join us. Together we could achieve so much."

"And if they're not friendly?"

Donovan shrugged. "Then we'll locate a suitable island and put them ashore before we sink their ship."

"Is that necessary?"

"We can't permit them to repair their sub if they are antagonistic towards us. They would be tempted to try and destroy us later on. If they're hostile, that sub goes down."

Alex gazed at the viewscreen. "Their executive officer sounded like a reasonable man."

"Yes, he did."

"Too bad there weren't enough reasonable men and women around when the world needed them."

"*Charkov* is starting to rise," Dave Jennings stated. "Speed is barely one knot."

"Try not to lose her, Mr. Hooper," Donovan quipped.

A ripple of laughter spread around the bridge, an indication that the tension had dissipated, that the crew was beginning to relax after their nerve-racking ordeal.

"I'll try, sir," Hooper responded with a grin.

Donovan allowed himself the luxury of a genuine smile and scanned the bridge, proud of his men, of their performance during their first engagement. He focused on the communications officer and saw

Jennings stiffen. "Something wrong, Mr. Jennings?"

"I'm not sure, Captain."

"Can you be more specific?"

"Sonar had an echo there for a moment."

"Another ship?"

"Yes, sir. But the depth reading was—" Jennings said, and abruptly checked his statement. His next words electrified the entire bridge crew. "Captain, it's *Nemesis!*"

24

Donovan came out of his chair in a rush and took several strides toward the communications officer. "Nemesis!" he exclaimed, the word almost a feral snarl, his usually cool composure shattered. He glanced at the screen and saw her, a small icon becoming larger quickly, her position to the southeast of the *Charkov*, rising out of the inky depths like a killer whale going after helpless prey.

"Range is seven thousand yards. Speed is fifty-two knots. Depth, twenty-four hundred feet."

"She's making straight for the Russians," Percy noted.

"And the *Charkov* is between *Nemesis* and us," Donovan snapped. "Mr. Hooper, take us around the Russian sub. Heading two-four-zero. Ahead all full."

"Ahead all full, Captain."

"Mr. Jennings, open a line to the Russians."

"Hailing them, Captain."

Donovan waited impatiently for the link to be established, clenching his fists at his sides, watching *Nemesis* grow nearer to the Soviet attack sub.

Jennings turned and offered a headset. "Here, sir."

His fingers flying, Donovan donned the headset. "Captain Donovan here. Who's this?"

"Executive Officer Dragominov, Captain."

"There's no time to explain, but your ship is in great danger. There's another sub bearing down on you from the southeast."

"Another sub?" Dragominov repeated. "Just a moment. Our sonar is operating erratically."

"There's no time to waste!" Donovan declared urgently. "Take my word for it. We've had run-ins with this sub before. You *must* reach the surface as fast as you can. We'll try to intercept her before she attacks."

"We will try."

Dragominov handed the microphone back to the communications operator and hurried over to Porfori. Could this be an American trick? he wondered. If so, what point would it serve? The American commander had sounded genuinely concerned. "What is the status of our sonar?"

"It comes and goes, Comrade."

"There is another submarine approaching from the southeast. Find it."

"I will."

"Helmsman Kuprevici, push our batteries to the limit. Get us to the surface."

"Right away, Comrade."

Frowning, Dragominov stared at the deck, at the four centimeters of water still underfoot. The pumps were working sluggishly, but they would have the water cleared out in fifteen minutes or less. He noticed a pair of seamen carrying Political Officer Vatutin from the control room.

"Comrade, I have it!" the sonar operator stated. "Distance to the target is five thousand, two hundred meters. The sub is closing rapidly. Fifty-eight knots." He paused. "They are below us. Depth approximately seven hundred meters."

"Damn. Helmsman, what is our speed?"

"Twenty-seven knots and climbing, Comrade."

"Faster. We must go faster."

Kuprevici nodded and applied himself to the task, exasperated because the helm responded so sluggishly. The tone in his superior's voice had convinced him of the urgency of the situation. He took pride in his competence, and he nursed the vessel higher with all the skill at his command.

Who was this other submarine? Dragominov mused. Why was it attacking? Clearly, the sub could not be American if the *Liberator* had fought him. Chinese, perhaps? German, maybe? Or even Iranian. Soviet Naval Intelligence had reported that Iran had put a submarine into service only the year before, thanks in large measure to technological assistance from the Chinese and the French. No one knew whether the Iranian submarine was nuclear powered or conventional.

"The other sub is still closing, Comrade," the sonar operator reported. "The American sub is speeding around to our port side."

"Can you get a screw signature on the other sub?"

"I have tried, but my equipment must not be functioning properly."

"Why is that?"

"Because the screw signatures on both ships are identical."

The revelation bewildered Dragonimov. Identical screw signatures normally meant identical ships. But how could this be? Was the second sub American after all?

"Range to the other sub is now five thousand meters."

"Comrade Kuprevici, what is our speed?"

"Thirty-five knots and rising."

Dragominov could feel his abdomen tighten. "Can we get a firing solution on the second sub?"

"Negative, Comrade. Even if we could, we have

221

no power in the torpedo room. We cannot open the outer torpedo tube doors."

Gritting his teeth, Dragominov suppressed an impulse to hit something. They were defenseless, at the mercy of the mystery sub. Ironically, their only hope lay in the *Liberator*. He almost laughed at the absurdity of it all. Captain Vazov had had the right idea all along. Life *was* a lesson in lunacy. The madness never would end.

"Thirty-eight knots," Helmsman Kuprevici divulged.

Still too slow, Dragominov realized. The second sub would fire at any moment. He hoped they were not Iranians. To be killed by a bunch of rabid fanatics was not his idea of a fitting demise for a Soviet officer.

Hold on.

Dragominov's forehead creased as he abruptly remembered a report that had crossed Vazov's desk several months ago, a report that might have a bearing on the identity of the attacking ship. He swiveled toward the radio operator. "Contact the *Liberator* again. I want to speak to their captain."

"Right away, Comrade."

Before the line could be opened, however, the sonar operator called out, "Torpedo in the water. Speed is sixty-eight knots. Range, four thousand, seven hundred meters."

Dragominov cursed. "Helmsman, take evasive action."

"Nemesis has launched a torpedo," Communications Officer Jennings stated coldly. "Distance between the fish and the Russian sub is just under three miles."

"What's our distance to the fish?" Donovan asked.

"Three and a half miles, Captain."

"We're going to try to get close enough to jam that torpedo," Donovan stated.

"*Nemesis* is starting to dive again," Jennings said.

"She's not even staying around to verify her kill," Donovan noted.

"She must not want any part of us," Percy mentioned.

Donovan nodded his agreement. *Nemesis* still seemed intent on playing her little game of hide-and-seek. But why? What the hell was *Liberator*'s twin trying to prove? The attack on the *Charkov* made about as much sense as the nuking of the Japanese fishing fleet. Both acts were irrational.

Or were they?

Everywhere *Liberator* went, *Nemesis* followed. Either *Nemesis* possessed better sensing equipment or someone on board *Nemesis* was psychic, because *Nemesis* was always one jump ahead of *Liberator*. *Nemesis* invariably seemed to know *Liberator*'s position before *Liberator*'s sensing equipment even detected her presence. *Nemesis* had already demonstrated her slightly superior speed and diving capability. Perhaps, given her past performance, *Nemesis* was once again trying to prove her preeminence. In that light, the attacks on the fishing boats and the Russian sub did make a bizarre sort of sense.

If *Nemesis* had been lying off the California coast during *Liberator*'s stay at San Francisco, *Nemesis* undoubtedly knew about the nuclear strike Donovan had called on the white-shirts. Whoever manned *Nemesis* had undoubtedly detected the explosion on their sensors. And if they were intent on demonstrating that *Nemesis* could match or exceed *Liberator* in every respect, they might have nuked the fishing fleet as evidence of their power. By the same token, *Nemesis* might have monitored the progress of the battle between *Liberator* and the *Charkov* from a safe distance and the commander of the enigmatic vessel had decided to show that *Nemesis* was every bit the equal of *Liberator* when it came to disposing of Soviet attack subs.

The line of reasoning disturbed Donovan. If the commander of *Nemesis* was truly trying to show that anything *Liberator* could do, *Nemesis* could do better, then the otherwise baffling behavior indicated that a madman must be commanding the phantom sub. Either that or a four-year-old.

"Captain, the *Charkov* is taking evasive measures," Communications Officer Jennings stated. "But she's only doing forty knots."

"Initiate jamming procedures against that torpedo."

"Beginning jamming procedures."

Donovan pivoted toward the Cyclops display, his features downcast. He doubted the jamming would be effective. Not when they were so far away. And not when the torpedo was locked on the distinctive sounds *Charkov* made. The homing computer on the fish would automatically ignore the jamming pulses if they deviated in the slightest degree from the pulses emitted by the torpedo. On the screen the torpedo streaked like an arrow toward the Russian sub.

Alex came from around the captain's chair, her gaze on the tableau unfolding on the viewscreen. "Isn't there anything else we can do?"

Donovan shook his head.

"Captain, the *Charkov* is trying to raise us again, but the transmission keeps breaking up."

"Answer them. Tell them they're breaking up."

"Yes, sir."

"Can't you try the laser?" Alex asked anxiously.

"Mr. Jennings, advise Weapons Control to try and stop the torpedo once it's within laser range."

"Advising, Captain."

"Any results on the jamming?"

"No, sir. Not yet."

"Have you established contact with the *Char-kov?*"

"Not yet."

"How close are we to the Russian sub?"

"Not quite a thousand yards due east."

There was nothing left to do but watch and wait. Donovan thought it strange that here he was rooting for the Soviets to elude the torpedo when only a short while ago he had been attempting to send the *Charkov* to the bottom. None of the Russian evasive tactics had succeeded in throwing the fish off course. Inevitably, with impeccable precision and increasing speed, the torpedo closed the gap. *Liberator* swept well past the Russian sub and drew within fifteen hundred yards of the fish.

Donovan smiled when Weapons Control cut loose with the laser, and for a few brief seconds he entertained the notion that the strategy would succeed. But each burst of the blue-green light missed by several yards.

"Oh, God," Alex said when it became apparent that there was no stopping the torpedo.

"Captain, I have Executive Officer Dragominov on the horn," Jennings said.

"On the speaker again," Donovan directed, and straightened. "This is Donovan. Can you hear me?"

Crisp static crackled over the air for a bit, and then the Russian came on, his voice breaking up as he spoke. "This is Dragominov. I can hear you. There is something I must—" The remainder of his sentence was lost to more static.

"I didn't catch that," Donovan stated. "Come again?"

The interference persisted for all of five seconds.

225

"—screw signatures. I know the identity of the other sub," Dragominov said.

The surprising revelation jolted Donovan. "Who are they? How do you know?"

Instead of a response, the crackling increased in volume while on the holographic display a finger's width separated the *Charkov* from the torpedo.

"Dragominov, are you there? Can you read me?"

"—systems are failing. Listen, Donovan. As one seaman to another, as one officer to another, as men who were made enemies by circumstance rather than design, I ask you to destroy the bastards for us. Do not let us die in vain. I see it all so clearly now. They are to blame, Donovan. They are our true enemy."

"Who, Dragominov? *Who are they?*"

"They are—"

Liberator's entire crew heard the devastating explosion through the hull. From the speaker emanated an inarticulate cry, then a few shrieks in the background followed by tremendous metallic tearing sounds and a vaporous hissing. Depicted in brilliant hues of red and orange on Cyclops, the blast ripped the Russian submarine in half amidships and from there the water pressure did the rest. The remaining bulkheads crumpled as compartment after compartment was vented to the sea. Both sections immediately began to sink, the stern section tumbling slowly end over end. The bow section tilted almost vertical, then dropped toward the murky depths below.

In the silence that descended on the bridge, Donovan felt a conflicting swirl of emotions. Those men had tried to kill him, hadn't they? They had tried to destroy his ship. So why did he feel an overpowering sorrow? Why was he filled with an intense hatred of *Nemesis?* Why did he have the feeling he had just lost a potential ally in his effort to salvage

226

what remained of the world? He bowed his head and moved to his chair, weariness pervading his being.

"Are you okay, Tom?" Alex inquired.

"Fine," Donovan replied. Her question made him aware of the dejected image he must be presenting to the crew. He sat down, his chin held high, and cleared his throat. "Mr. Hooper, we will resume our original course to the Gilbert Islands. Ahead one-third."

"Aye, Captain."

"Mr. Jennings, any sign of *Nemesis?*"

"No, sir."

"Too bad. I'm in the mood to kick some ass."

25

They stood hand in hand in the middle of the fore-deck and admired the resplendent hues cast by the setting sun. On the topside bridge, the lookout studiously avoided training his binoculars in their direction.

"Tomorrow we begin our sweep of the Gilberts," Alex commented, studying Donovan's features.

"Yeah."

"Keep your fingers crossed. We could find the base you need."

"Maybe."

"Want to talk about it?"

"What?"

"Whatever is bothering you."

Donovan glanced at her. "Nothing is—" he began, then sighed and shook his head. "No, that would be lying. You're right. Something is bothering me."

"The Russian sub?"

"The *Charkov* is part of it. I liked the sound of that guy Dragominov. I only talked to him for a few minutes, and yet he impressed me as being sane and open-minded. He wasn't a rabid warmonger."

"Speaking of warmongers, at least Percy is now willing to concede that the Russians might not have started the war."

"There's hope for the world after all," Donovan quipped.

Alex grinned and gave his hand a squeeze. "What else is bothering you?"

"*Nemesis.*"

"I should have guessed."

"I'm starting to believe that a madman must be at her helm. Whoever it is, they seem determined to constantly be a thorn in our side," Donovan said, and paused, staring thoughtfully at the western horizon. "Or do they?"

"I don't follow you."

"Do you realize that not once has *Nemesis* fired a torpedo at us?"

"So?"

"We've fired three fish at her. One was almost a direct hit. Yet they haven't taken any aggressive action against us. Why not? What if I've misjudged them? What if *Nemesis* was never a threat in the first place?"

"If they're not a threat, why haven't they attempted to contact you? Why haven't they identified themselves?"

"I don't know."

"Why do they keep playing these senseless games with you?"

Donovan sighed. "I wish I knew."

"You have the lives of your crew to think of. You can't afford to let down your guard for a minute," Alex said. She pecked him on the cheek. "Is it my imagination, or are you having a lot of second thoughts lately?"

"I guess I am," Donovan admitted.

"Why?"

"Maybe it's all catching up with me," Donovan responded wearily. "It's been one thing after another since the war, and I've been so busy fulfilling my duties as captain that I haven't had a lot of time to come to grips with everything personally. I'm not even sure I've come to terms with the deaths of my parents."

Alex said nothing, simply listened, allowing him to air his suppressed feelings, intuitively sensing the turmoil within him.

"I had such high hopes, Alex. When *Liberator* came out from under the polar ice and we discovered the world had committed the ultimate insanity, I envisioned our role as being a rescue ship. Our mission would be to look for survivors and salvage what we could from the wreckage of civilization. I think in the back of my mind that I assumed the worst was over, that any survivors would all be working toward the common goal of rebuilding our shattered lives," Donovan said, and frowned. "Little did I realize how wrong my perspective was until we began to hunt for survivors. The white-shirts attacked us. *Nemesis* began dogging our every move. Even the animals are rising up against humanity and reclaiming the land we once dominated. Nature herself is against us."

"You found survivors in San Francisco," Alex reminded him.

Donovan smiled wanly and kissed her forehead. "For which I will be eternally grateful. But you see my point, don't you? The war *isn't* over. The meaningless violence *hasn't* ended. In fact, the worst may be yet to come. The lucky ones may have been those who were killed in the first nuclear blasts." He reached up and rubbed the back of his neck. "I was wrong. *Liberator*'s primary mission will still be that of a warship. The Russians are still fighting World War Three, and everywhere we go we'll have to be on the watch for them. We have no way of knowing who else is lurking out there, waiting for the chance to blow us out of the water."

"No one ever said it would be easy."

"You think I don't know that?" Donovan replied. "You think I don't realize we'll be lucky if we're still around ten years from now? Hell, five years. We'll be fortunate if we accomplish any lasting good at all."

"Is that what this is all about? You're worried that all we do will be in vain?"

The insight made him do a double take, and for half a minute his expression shifted and rippled as he came to terms with his personal demons of self-doubt and remorse. Finally a wry smile creased his lips. He leaned down and kissed her. "Thank you."

"For what?"

"For your support, your caring. You're right, of course. Any good we accomplish must count for something. And since no one else is around to take the mantle of re-creating the world on their shoulders, it's up to us."

"Adam and Eve, huh?"

"Something like that."

Alex beamed. "I knew you weren't a quitter, Thomas P. Donovan. But you do look a little peaked."

"I am tired, Alex. So very, very tired. I'd like to crawl into the sack and stay there for a week."

"Now there's an idea I can live with. How would you like some company?" Alex proposed impishly.

"Sound great to me, but the crew might talk."

"Let them."

True to Alex's prediction, the Gilbert Islands turned out to be unsuitable for *Liberator*'s base. Nowhere could they find the natural deep-water port Donovan insisted was necessary for a safe haven, and after the incident with the Russian attack sub he was not about to compromise one bit. They spent several days going from island to island, taking their time, recuperating from their ordeal. The spirits of the crew, which had fallen to a distressing low after *Nemesis* destroyed the *Charkov,* rebounded.

Three more active volcanoes were discovered, one of which had completely obliterated Christmas Island. They found several deserted towns and settlements, not to mention over a dozen abandoned native villages with the houses still intact. Donovan permitted the crew to go ashore in shifts on one of the islands for some badly needed rest and relaxation.

Alex went with Donovan and the last shift. Together they inspected the homes in a small village near the sandy shore, going from building to building, marveling at the simplicity of the life the islanders enjoyed. In a few houses they found cooking pots filled with decaying food, evidence that the natives had departed in great haste.

After checking the village they walked to the beach and strolled along the water's edge.

Donovan inhaled deeply and motioned at the serene setting. "This is just what we needed to return us to normal."

"You *are* a changed man."

"We all have moody spells now and then."

"So what's our next move, fearless leader? On to the Society Islands?"

"Yep. You've maintained all along that they are our best bet. I'm eager to get there."

The patter of footsteps on the sand sounded to their rear and they turned.

"Hope I'm not disturbing you two lovebirds," Charlie declared as he joined them.

"What's up, Pirate?" Donovan queried.

"I wanted to ask Alex a question."

"Ask away," Alex said.

"Okay," Charlie responded, his countenance a study in earnest consideration. "You're our expert on the South Pacific, right?"

"By default, I suppose. Yes, why?"

"Do you speak any of the native dialects?"

"Not a one," Alex said.

"Do we have any of the languages on file in the computer?"

"No. We have all the historical information concerning the various island chains, though. Would that help?"

"Nope," Charlie said, and stared wistfully at the village. "Afraid not."

"Why this sudden interest in the native dialects?" Donovan inquired.

"Well, the way I figure, it's only a matter of time before we find an inhabited island. They can't *all* be deserted."

"Yeah. So?"

"So, big brother, it may not have occurred to you, since you have Alex and all, but some of us are in desperate need of human companionship. If you get my drift."

Donovan grinned. "I think I do."

"I want to be prepared when we finally find more natives. That's where I hoped Alex would come in handy."

"How?"

"By teaching me how to say a few basic sentences in Micronesian."

"What sentences?" Donovan deliberately probed with a wink at Alex.

"Oh, you know," Charlie said, and shifted his feet.

"No, I don't know. Enlighten me."

"The basics, big brother. Things like 'You have a great body.' 'Your eyes are lovely.' 'Your skin is as smooth as silk' 'Give me back my underwear.' Those sort of sentences."

For the first time in weeks, Captain Thomas Donovan threw back his head and laughed uproariously.

"You're not going to sail to our new home in a twenty-seven-foot boat," Alex said with undisguised horror.

"Why not?"

"Because these are shark-filled waters!"

"Where's your sense of adventure?"

"Back in the computer library. I read about adventure, Donovan. I don't do it."

"Is this the woman I remember as commander of the Survivors in San Francisco? Packing a pistol and all that?"

"I've retired," she said. "I realize that my true value is in research and development. I'm hard at work designing a habitat for living, to be used once we find a new home."

"Make sure the one you design for you and me has a dock," Donovan insisted. "I intend to take the Corsair with us."

"You can't sail there. You have to steer the submarine."

"Hooper steers the submarine. I just sit behind him and play coach. Anyway, Mr. Jennings is an old sailor as well as a would-be bar owner. He's volunteered to sail her. And it won't take him long—the Corsair will do fifteen knots easily. We'll need a fast coastal sailboat once we're established on the island. What's the name of that island?"

"Espiritu. I don't know why you can't remember the name."

"Don't have to. My science officer remembers things for me. Hand me another Coke, would you?"

She pulled a bottle out of the Styrofoam cooler that had been set up on the porch of the Royal Tahitian Yacht Club and handed it to him, top off. He sipped it as he watched the first party come ashore from *Liberator,* looking like sailors always did when being turned loose on an island Paradise: both eager and apprehensive.

"I hope those guys don't get into too much trouble," he said.

"They shouldn't. Half of them are Ph.D's, for God's sake, and the rest have advanced engineering degrees. This is hardly your stereotypical Navy crew. Probably they'll fix the water supply and detoxify the fruit."

Dr. Peter Fisher came out onto the porch carrying a stack of reports and helped himself to a soda and a chair.

"I have some good news," he said, putting his feet up on a chair.

"Let's hear it."

"The contaminated fruit is no good and will have to be thrown out. But the stuff now growing on the trees is okay. The toxins apparently pass quickly through the surface soils and dissolve in the rock strata."

"Then the poisoning is transient!" Alex said, excitedly.

"It should be. The trees have already regained health and are producing edible fruit. The water supply will be okay once it's flushed. In short, there should be no problem in our living in the South Pacific indefinitely."

"Sensational!" Donovan said, and paused to radio the news to Percy on the ship and Chief Smith, who commanded a party working to flush the city's water system. A moment later, a radio relay caused a whoop of delight to go up from the shore party. The word that it was safe to live in the islands spread quickly.

"Now all we have to do is find an island," Donovan said.

"We can't use this one," Dr. Fisher said. "At least not until I find out what happened to the population."

"We can't use it anyway. Tahiti is too well-known. Enemies—and we have to assume there are many of them out there—will be able to find us. Espiritu is sounding better and better."

"And only a two-day sail for *Priscilla*. That means that the Corsair can make it in under a day."

"What's the Corsair?" Dr. Fisher asked.

"My boat," Donovan announced.

"I thought your boat was *Liberator*."

"That's my *ship*. I know that it's a fine distinction—boat and ship—but one you'll grow to understand. Carry on, Doctor."

"That means get back to work," Alex interpreted.

"I'll see if I can figure out what happened to the Tahitians," Dr. Fisher sniffed, returning to his lab setup inside the club.

"Come with me," Donovan said, taking Alex by the hand and leading her off the porch and in the direction of pier three.

The Corsair was three hulls wide and only twenty-seven feet long, but designed as a fast racer with ocean-crossing ability. Twenty-seven feet was indeed short for extended sailing in shark-infested waters, but she did have a cabin that slept four—two in comfort—and she was fast. One experienced man could sail her, and for two it was a breeze. Donovan figured she would be useful for running errands around their new home . . . going down the coast to look for something, or making short island hops.

Donovan helped Alex into the cockpit, which stretched ten feet from the transom to the companionway door. The cockpit was crammed with racing equipment—hydraulic boom vang and downhaul, self-tailing winches, and more navigation equipment than you could shake a stick at. The boat was equipped for a trans-Pacific crossing, with a fresh water distiller and solar panels on the cabin top that made electricity for the batteries. Everything about her said speed and ease of handling.

The companionway door swung open to reveal a well-stocked cabin and a double-sized bunk. Donovan hooked his fingers under her belt and pulled her to him.

"Welcome to the *Corsair,*" he said. "I decided to keep the name."

"You have a thing about making love on boats," she said, not resisting at all.

"My mom and dad lived on one when I was a little kid. It used to rock me to sleep."

"That's my job now," Alex replied, whipping off her sweat shirt to free her breasts to the salt air.

At midnight the yacht club glowed merrily. The second shore party was reveling in the still tropical night. Their lights and those of *Liberator* out in the harbor were nearly all there were, apart from a three-quarter moon and stars. The Southern Cross hung over a Papeete where only automatic street lights glowed and the only men and woman stirring were submariners.

True, there were animals about. Dogs and cats came out from hiding with the evening. Lizards

240

skittered about as did land crabs and, after night-fall, the cries of birds filled the air. But people . . . there was no sign of them, and their absence grew more and more surreal as the night wore on.

Alex fell asleep early and slept like a rock. She was still dead to the world when the boat's chronometer struck eight bells for midnight. Donovan covered her with a cotton sheet and wandered up onto the dock, where the muted sound of music caught his ear.

Charlie sat on a mooring post listening to a compact disc player and staring out to sea. The player sat on the dock.

"Where'd you get that?" Donovan asked.

"I liberated it from a Tinito electronics shop a few blocks inland."

"Tinito?"

"Chinese. Don't worry—I left an I.O.U."

"I didn't see disc players on the shopping list of essential items."

"Music is essential. It's the one thing this crew is missing, other than women, and they're due tomorrow on *Priscilla.*"

Donovan smiled. "The music rings a bell."

"It's the Stones fortieth anniversary disc—a real oldie. Dad had one like it. I remember he used to sit on the bow of the *West Wind* and play it."

"Sounds good. Then again, I always did have old-fashioned tastes."

"Alex is asleep?"

"Yeah I wish I could sleep like that. You could set off a bomb out here and she wouldn't wake up."

"Not that there's anything here to make noise. This crew ain't exactly a party crew. They have fun, but *really.*"

"What are they doing?"

"There's a hot poker game raging up in the yacht club. At the same table men have played poker for

241

a hundred years. My sense is that nothing has changed."

Donovan offered a quizzical look.

"Since the war, I mean," his brother went on. "Everything and nothing have changed. We're still here, and we're still doing the stuff men have always done. Play poker, stand guard over sleeping women, and stare out to sea."

"Funny that we spend all our time at sea looking toward land, and when we get to land we turn around and look out to sea."

"Not exactly a profound or original thought, big brother," Charlie said.

"Like you said, nothing changes. Have the lookouts reported any sightings?"

"Not a damn thing. There's a couple of cats fighting over on the Boulevard Pomore and a couple of dogs barking at them, but other than that, all is quiet."

"If the natives are around, they ain't showing themselves. We haven't exactly kept a low profile." He nodded in the direction of *Liberator*'s mooring lights, which glowed across the harbor. "They must be dead."

"They're not dead," Charlie said authoritatively.

"How do you know?"

"I don't know. But they're out there in the jungle."

"Doing what?"

"Wandering around. I don't know. It's just a feeling."

The disc player had come to the end of one side, and he paused to reset it. Then from out of the silence came a crack of wood on wood and a splash.

"Oars!" he said. "Out there!" He pointed out to the darkness beyond the ghostly shadow of *Liberator*.

Donovan strained to see in the darkness but could

242

find nothing. The sound persisted . . . a couple of cracks and splashes, then silence, then another sound of wood on wood.

That was followed by a shout from the watch officer on *Liberator* and the flicking on of a powerful spotlight that shot down from the topside bridge and cut a swatch across the harbor.

Donovan and Charlie raced down the dock to where one of the inflatables was tied up, jumped inside, and revved up the engine. Soon Donovan was pushing the powerful outboard hard into the night while Charlie stood on the bow holding a Franchi.

Donovan whipped out his portable transceiver and spoke into it! "Captain to *Liberator* . . . we're heading out in the inflatable. What's going on?"

"One of the double-hulled canoes, Captain," was the reply. "It came fast out of the far shore of the harbor. There was no warning."

"Where is it now?"

"Dead ahead of you. Two hundred yards."

Charlie yelled back, "I can't see a thing."

"How come we didn't pick it up on sensors? What the hell was Communications doing?"

"I got it now! Slow down!"

Donovan eased off on the throttle and the outboard motor calmed to a gentle, purring roar as the small boat came off its plane and settled down into the still harbor water. At the same time, *Liberator*'s spotlight picked out the twin-hulled piroque.

It lay in the darkness, ghostly in the spotlight, a solitary man standing in the starboard hull, a paddle in his hand. He wore a loincloth that seemed to have been fashioned out of khaki.

"What the hell?" Donovan said, to himself, really.

The intruder hefted the paddle as if it were a spear and threw it at the inflatable.

243

His aim was poor. The paddle splashed down four or five feet to one side of its target. Charlie raised the Franchi, then lowered the gun when he saw that the intruder had hurled his only weapon and was standing staring, an odd, lost look on his Polynesian face.

The sea gave forth an explosion of water and the piroque rocked violently to one side as the dark dorsal skin of a gigantic shark smashed into it. The man tumbled into the water and disappeared immediately, torn in half by the four sharks that followed the first.

"Jesus fucking Christ!" Donovan yelled.

"Let's get outta here!" Charlie yelled back.

Donovan revved the engine back up and turned the inflatable hard to port.

His radio spoke: "Captain, sensors picking up sharks."

"We found them!" he shouted, and turned the boat toward *Liberator*.

The big shark that overturned the piroque turned on the inflatable, racing at it and striking it a glancing blow, rows of gleaming white teeth raking along the starboard side as Donovan turned the outboard away from it. Charlie shouted and a burst of automatic weapons fire tore into the creature. Two smaller sharks approached from the bow and he turned away from them too, the raft zigzagging toward *Liberator* amidst a sea of gleaming teeth and dorsal fins.

"There's sharks all over!" Charlie yelled, looking back as a wolf pack of small sharks attacked the blood scent on the big one he had shot up.

On *Liberator* men poured out onto the deck, Franchis and other guns at the ready. Three flares shot into the sky and illuminated the night. Another crew stood by the side, ready to take the inflatable on board.

In the growing light as the inflatable raced up to the hull of the submarine, Donovan could see the harbor almost carpeted with sharks. Their dorsals sliced the surface into a foam and their teeth slashed at the thin hull of the fleeing raft. Another big one zoomed in front of the inflatable and Donovan gunned the engine so that the raft skittered over it, the propeller cutting a row of slices into its back.

Donovan ran straight at the hull of *Liberator* in between two rows of automatic weapons fire as his men shot into the water to drive off the predators. White hands grabbed at the raft and hauled it aboard. Charlie and Donovan scrambled up onto the foredeck, hearing teeth gnash at the hull and weapons tear into angry black bodies.

Donovan turned to the sea and stared, astonished. As far as the spotlights could go, the water roiled with twisting sharks.

"Holy shit," Charlie said.

"All hands get below!" Donovan yelled. He chased them all down the hatches and scrambled to the bridge. "Emergency dive, straight down far enough to submerge the laser ports!"

"Aye, Captain."

He could feel the ship settling underneath him and watched the Cyclops display the depth. When the keel nearly touched the harbor bottom, *Liberator* stopped.

Donovan ordered, "Lasers on full power, three hundred and sixty degree dispersion . . . repetitive fire!"

The blue-green lasers fired from hull-mounted ports fore and aft of the sail and swept the underwater horizon, using a design feature meant to clear mine fields. As the beams shot through the sea they tore up the marauding sharks, missing most but killing a few and wounding enough to turn the others upon them.

The firing lasted only ten seconds but the carnage continued for an hour. Eventually, *Liberator* resurfaced and men went up on deck to watch it. Before half an hour had passed, Papeete harbor stunk with blood and entrails.

Charlie said, *"Canis lycaon."*

"What?"

"Timber wolves. We knew there were sharks in these waters, but this is fuckin' insane."

"The same as in San Francisco," Donovan agreed. "Yeah, I get your point. Man blew himself up, and the beasts continue to inherit the earth. I didn't really think it would extend to the sea."

FROM PERSONAL JOURNALS TO BLACKLY HUMOROUS ACCOUNTS

VIETNAM

DISPATCHES, Michael Herr
                    01976-0/$4.50 US/$5.95 Can
"I believe it may be the best personal journal about war,
any war, that any writer has ever accomplished."
        —Robert Stone, *Chicago Tribune*

M, John Sack
                    69866-8/$3.95 US/$4.95 Can
"A gripping and honest account, compassionate and
rich, colorful and blackly comic."
        —*The New York Times*

ONE BUGLE, NO DRUMS, Charles Durden
                    69260-0/$4.95 US/$5.95 Can
"The funniest, ghastliest military scenes put to paper
since Joseph Heller wrote *Catch-22*"
        —*Newsweek*

AMERICAN BOYS, Steven Phillip Smith
                    67934-5/$4.50 US/$5.95 Can
"The best novel I've come across on the war in Vietnam"
        —Norman Mailer

Avon Books presents your worst nightmares—

...haunted houses

ADDISON HOUSE   75587-4/$4.50 US/$5.95 Can
Clare McNally

THE ARCHITECTURE OF FEAR
                          70553-2/$3.95 US/$4.95 Can
edited by Kathryn Cramer & Peter D. Pautz

...unspeakable evil

HAUNTING WOMEN   89881-0/$3.95 US/$4.95 Can
edited by Alan Ryan

TROPICAL CHILLS   75500-9/$3.95 US/$4.95 Can
edited by Tim Sullivan

...blood lust

THE HUNGER   70441-2/$4.50 US/$5.95 Can
THE WOLFEN   70440-4/$4.50 US/$5.95 Can
Whitley Strieber

WORLD WAR II
Edwin P. Hoyt

STORM OVER THE GILBERTS: 63651-4/$3.50 US/$4.50 Can
War in the Central Pacific: 1943
The dramatic reconstruction of the bloody battle over the Japanese-held Gilbert Islands.

CLOSING THE CIRCLE: 67983-8/$3.50 US/$4.95 Can
War in the Pacific: 1945
A behind-the-scenes look at the military and political moves drawn from official American and Japanese sources.

McCAMPBELL'S HEROES   68841-7/$3.95 US/$5.75 Can
A stirring account of the daring fighter pilots, led by Captain David McCampbell, of Air Group Fifteen.

LEYTE GULF   75408-8/$3.50 US/$4.50 Can
The Death of the Princeton
The true story of a bomb-torn American aircraft carrier fighting a courageous battle for survival!

WAR IN THE PACIFIC: TRIUMPH OF JAPAN
          75792-3/$4.50 US/$5.50 Can

WAR IN THE PACIFIC: STIRRINGS   75793-1/$3.95 US/$4.95 Can

THE JUNGLES OF NEW GUINEA   75750-8/$4.95 US/$5.95 Can